Shadows from the Sky

EVA SEYLER

Library of Congress Control Number: 2023910106

Typeset in Cormorant and Quintessential

E-Book ISBN: 979-8-9880877-2-4
Paperback ISBN: 979-8-9880877-1-7
Audiobook ISBN: 979-8-9880877-3-1

For Jen
because of the aeroplanes

and for Molly
in spite of them

Flying is the best possible thing for women.

Raymonde de la Roche, 1882-1919

Life is like a landscape.

*You live in the midst of it but can describe it only
from the vantage point of distance.*

Charles Lindbergh, 1902-1974

*You haven't seen a tree until you've seen its shadow
from the sky.*

Amelia Earhart, 1897-1939

SALEM, OREGON: 1927

I want to fly.

My mother says it's dangerous and not very ladylike.

My best friend George doesn't care about the ladylike bit, but he also says it's dangerous, and likes to point out to me every time the papers report another aviation-related accident or fatality.

But I still want to fly, and someday I will.

It's not fame I want. *Definitely* not the worship the entire country has given Colonel Charles Lindbergh, ever since he crossed the Atlantic at the end of May.

What I want is something else entirely.

I remember the exact day it began, when George and I were ten and still lived in Turner, a tiny town about eight miles southeast of here. We ran away from home that day, hopping a train like hoboes. (It was one of my more stupid ideas. I know. I was just really mad at my evil stepfather, okay? And George is nothing if not my loyal shadow. And I so desperately wanted to be *free*.)

It was a Monday, the twenty-ninth of June. The train we hopped took us right up here, to Salem, where we spent the afternoon wandering and used some of the money I'd brought along to see a picture called *The Air Mail*. That's how I remember the date, because I found the ticket stub in my pocket later and pasted it into a scrapbook. *The Air Mail* was magical and I've never forgotten how it made me feel. It showed me freedom.

George, who currently cares only about WORDS and THEOLOGY and HEBREW SYNTAX (whatever that means), has apparently forgotten that, at the time, he agreed with me that the picture was "swell". I'd thought I wanted to be president of the United States when I grew up, but *The Air Mail* changed my mind. Ever since, I've only wanted to be a pilot.

To *fly*.

Fly free like a bird.

It was my mother who, indirectly, inspired me to write down this story of all that happened this year, although I haven't told her so and don't plan to show this to her or anyone for a very long time, if ever. It has been such an odd year, and I might forget some of the details if I don't get it written down while it's all fresh in my mind.

Because it's a good story. Good enough for a book, I think. And I guess I can always come back later and get it all fixed up. (My spelling is terrible.)

It all began at my house in Turner, on the first Saturday in March, this year: 1927.

MARCH 5, 1927: SATURDAY

I woke up from a dream about a telephone that wouldn't stop ringing to a silent house where the telephone definitely wasn't ringing.

But something wasn't right, and I lay for a while in my pre-dawn-dim room, eyes still hazy with sleep, before I realized what it was.

The United States map on my wall, which greeted my eyes on waking every morning, wasn't there. I sat up quickly and leaned over my footboard to see it was in ragged pieces on the floor, with every last one of my aviator photos torn in half and tossed into the wreckage. Not even Bessie Coleman, my latest and most prized addition, had been excluded from this fate.

(After she died last year, I wrote to the airfield where it happened and begged them for a photograph, and someone very kindly sent me one and told me more about her too, which was fantastic because the paper here had barely any details.)

I dropped to my knees in front of the mess, eyes stinging with angry tears at this stupid destruction of my property, then sat back on my heels, thinking hard. My mother and I lived alone, and she would never have done this.

Someone had been in my room as I was sleeping.

It is a well-known fact that I fall asleep in an eyeblink and that even an apocalyptic hailstorm wouldn't rouse me, so the idea that someone might have come in unawares wasn't surprising. But I have very good reasons for fearing intruders, and the fear that filled me looking at this heap of torn paper was cold and terrible.

My door burst open, and my mother stood there, breathless, eyes wild and red-rimmed. She hadn't even put on her housecoat over her nightgown, a sure sign of severe agitation. (She is so very modest, even when it is only me here with her.)

"Pack your things," she said. "We're leaving this house."

I started to gesture towards the vandalism on my floor, but she had already vanished.

Besides being modest, my mother is an extremely retiring person; George calls her *fluttery*, and it's really a perfect description. She's gentle and pretty, but fragile like a butterfly. She doesn't say much at the best of times. I wish she would. I long to have a mother with whom I could talk confidentially anytime. But it always feels like there's some unseen barrier holding her back, just out of my reach.

I spend most of my time protecting her, honestly. After the disaster that was Sam, my stepfather, she's just... well, herself. But more so. Like a crumpled piece of waste paper that will skitter off into the wilderness if not carefully tended.

Anyway, it is not like Mother to come bursting into my room demanding I pack my things. She only did that one other time, for reasons I will explain later, so I knew something absolutely, monumentally *awful* must have happened. Something that hadn't anything to do with maps and aviators.

I pulled my father's old suitcase out from under my bed. I hadn't used it since last summer, when George and his dad took me to Scotland with them, and it was dusty. I wiped it off with my sleeve, opened it, and glanced around the room. Mother hadn't said how long we'd be away.

I stepped into the hall. "How much do I pack?" I hollered. "A week's worth? Less? More?"

"Everything we can fit into the car," her voice floated back to me from somewhere.

Okay then.

I took off my nightie, folded it into the suitcase, and got dressed for the day: long underwear and stockings under my dress and cardigan, topping it all off with one of my dead father's dark blue sweaters that I sometimes wore because it made him feel closer, and a sharp pang of longing for him overtook me, just for a moment. If only he was here now, so I could stop having to be so brave for my mother all by myself all the time!

6

I pulled myself together, tucking in my Sunday clothes, my party dress from George's Scottish aunt, Estelle, and as many other stockings and things would fit. I didn't forget my rag doll Clotilde. I had to sit on the case to get the latches to shut. Then I found a crate for my torn map and photos, and my schoolbooks and storybooks and pile of scrapbooks.

I heard Mother's footsteps up and down the stairs, slamming doors and drawers, dropping things, and occasionally sniffling.

Having finished my own packing, I brought my crate and suitcase to the front door and went to the kitchen to fry an egg for breakfast, since Mother seemed too preoccupied to be bothered with feeding her child and can't cook to save her life anyway. After the egg I had an orange and polished off the last of the milk in the icebox, thinking all the while about what could possibly have spooked Mother. Nothing else in the house seemed amiss or alarming.

She reappeared, flinging open the door to lug my suitcase out. I followed her to the car with my crate. The Buick's every spare inch

was crammed, including the secret compartment under the back seat where my bootlegging stepfather used to transport booze.

"You can't drive," I pointed out. "Why are we stuffing all this into the car?" I brightened. "Do *I* get to drive?"

She turned to look at me over her shoulder, wiping hair out of her eyes—pale, colorless hair like mine. Her eyes darted about. "No. No, you do not," she said decisively. "Mr. Graham is coming on the train. He's to drive us."

"What's going on, anyway?"

She ignored that. "Anything you want from here, you take now, because we're not coming back. We'll stay with the Grahams for a bit. And then..." she trailed off, shook her head as if to clear away cobwebs, and disappeared back into the house.

I was glad to hear Mr. Graham was coming, because staying with them meant I could finally be with George again. I'd missed him terribly since they left Turner for Salem last fall, right after Mr. G. and George and I got back from Scotland. The Grahams were our second-nearest neighbors when they lived in Turner, and that's partly how George got to be my best friend.

There are a lot of Grahams because they are, in the words of George's cousin Vincent, "prolific as rabbits". I have pictures of all of them in one of my scrapbooks. I'll list them here.

1. **George Graham**: my best friend, also twelve, but three months younger. His birthday is the 16th of December and I told him it's a shame he couldn't have waited just one more day and then he'd have come into the world on the anniversary of the Wright Brothers' first flight at Kitty Hawk, but he just rolled his eyes and said to take that up with his mother, as he had no say in the matter.

2. **Mrs. Graham**: George's mother, who said that she had no say in the matter, either.

3. **Mr. Graham**: George's father, who is a lawyer in Salem. He's gorgeous and knows it. Also wears terrible ties.

4. **Susan Graham**, now Susan Fleming: George's eldest

half-sister. Mr. Graham had four daughters with his first wife and it was Susan's wedding to a doctor named Robert that took us to Scotland last summer.

5-7. **Amanda, Mildred,** and **Beatrice,** the other of George's half-sisters: They live in England. Amanda's a teacher. Mildred is in her last year of school, and Beatrice is going to be an actress. She's going to a special school in London called the Royal Academy of Dramatic Art. George's uncle Jamie has a place in London and that's where she's living while she studies there. Not all by herself, of course! Aunt Estelle sent down a woman to take care of the house and look after her. Beatrice says she's quite grown up now (seventeen) and can take care of herself, but Aunt Estelle said if she didn't agree to the companion then she could just say goodbye to the Royal Academy, and Mr. Graham backed her up, so Beatrice had to give in. (The use of the London house is their contribution to her education there. Mr. Graham pays for some of her tuition, but most of the money comes out of the inheritance the girls got when their mother died.)

8. **Uncle Jamie Graham**: Mr. Graham's twin brother, who is the Earl of Inverlochy and lives in a CASTLE. I could go on and on about Uncle Jamie. But I'll do that later, maybe.

9-14. **Peter, Thomas, Vincent, Christopher, Gerald,** and **Genevieve:** Uncle Jamie's children. I will come back to them later. (Some of them.) (Mostly Vincent.)

15. **Aunt Estelle**: Uncle Jamie's beautiful, feisty, marvelous wife. I would like to be her when I grow up. *She* says she thinks me learning to fly planes sounds *simply topping*.

Inverlochy Castle, where Susan's wedding was, was enormous and magical and it is so hard for me to believe Mr. Graham actually was born and grew up there. He seems not so very different from anyone else. Uncle Jamie's children are so used to their surroundings

The Graham Family: Scottish Branch

I accumulated all these when we were
in Scotland last summer!

Peter (19) - Thomas (18) - Vincent (17)

Uncle Jamie and
Aunt Estelle

Christopher (7)

Gerald and Genevieve (5)
Look how adorable they are!

The Graham Family: English Branch

Susan (23) and Robert

Amanda (21)

Mildred (18)

Beatrice (17)

The Graham Family: American Branch

Mr and Mrs Graham
(George and Alice)

George (12)

that it just seems ordinary to them. They tear around it like a pack of wild dogs, completely unimpressed by the splendor. Me—well, I could never bring myself to swing down the spiral stairs on the rope like a monkey, or join the bicycle races down the portrait gallery's parquet floor, or any of the other madcap things they come up with.

Uncle Jamie, on the other hand, seems to belong in that castle, as if it's part of him.

But that's me rambling, so back to that day in March.

While my mother scooped armfuls of sheet music and hymnals from her beloved piano, I filled another box with some of our food, the stuff that needed to be used up soon: fruits and vegetables and the leftover roast beef from the previous night. (I will be charitable and not call it charred beef, which is more accurate.) I left everything else, because Mrs. Graham is Jewish and I couldn't remember all the things that were on her Not In My Kitchen list.

I found Mother on her piano bench, head resting on the keys, absolutely sobbing. I'd never seen her like this before, not even when Daddy died. She's always so buttoned-up. I knew she loved that piano, but it wasn't the only one in the world. Surely we'd be back, I thought, and she'd have it again.

"Are you going to get dressed?" I asked her, as gently as I could.

She startled, wiping her eyes, the grooves of middle D through G# impressed deep into her forehead, and glanced down as if surprised she was still in her nightgown. She flushed and fluttered off upstairs, where drawers and doors once again began slamming. I sat on the vacated bench and started playing *Mary Had a Little Lamb* in the style of Bach, one of many variations of the tune Mother had used to teach me to play, years ago. It was so familiar I didn't even have to think about it, unlike the most recent piece she'd assigned me, Schubert's *Moment Musicaux No. 3 in F Minor*. I brightened at the idea of a reprieve from daily piano practice. Not that I hated it, but I definitely would sooner have been doing other things, like tinkering with the car or designing airplanes out of wood scraps.

Eventually Mother returned, coat and hat on and gloves in hand. She paced, eyes flicking nervously from clock to front window and back again, pausing at the piano occasionally to caress its worn wood.

As soon as Mr. Graham bounded up the steps, before he had time to knock, Mother had the door open and pressed the car key into his hand. "Let's go," she said.

I stopped on the driveway at sight of my bicycle, propped up against the railing on the back porch. I looked at Mr. Graham, who had already put in the key and come back around front to crank it up. "Can I strap this on top?" I called over, indicating the bike.

He nodded and I ran to the shed for some rope. The two of us soon had it securely tied in place. Then I climbed in, sitting on Mother's lap because there wasn't room anywhere else. I could feel her tension in the anxious way she wrapped her arms around me, but Mr. Graham's silence alarmed me more. He is endlessly energetic and rarely shuts up, and when he does, it's usually in that irritating way grownups have when they think the child in their midst is not old enough to hear Important Adult Topics.

We arrived shortly before noon at what George had called the "Victorian monstrosity" in his letters to me. It was the house his mother had selected to buy while the rest of us were in Scotland, and it was exactly as appalling as I'd imagined, and so very, *very* salmon pink.

George was sitting on the front steps watching for us and beat his father to letting us out.

"Wow, that's a lot of stuff," he said, eyeing the loaded car.

"Hi to you too," I said, and he grinned.

For a few seconds we stood awkwardly, saying nothing, until Mr. Graham pressed two dollar bills into George's hand and told us to scram for a bit. This immediately made me suspicious and inclined to eavesdrop under a window, but George, whose lack of curiosity is SO DEPLORABLE it took *my* digging two years ago to find out about Mr. Graham's four older daughters (and wife!) still living in England, just stuffed the money into his pocket and turned away from the house.

(I should add that by the time all of these secrets came out, the wife had died, so George's mother could become really *truly* Mrs. Graham after so many years of living in sin just *pretending* to be Mrs.

Graham, and that did a great deal towards brightening her out of the dull slump she was in when I first knew her.)

George said, "Did you bring a coat or are you planning to just wear that... thing?"

I looked down. "This 'thing' is Daddy's and I like it, and no, I did not bring another coat."

"Okay," he said with a slight shrug. "Hat?"

I shook my head, and he ran inside to fetch me one of his mother's warm wool hats. I pulled it over my head, grateful. It was very damp out. "Where are we scramming to?" I asked.

"Where'd you like to scram to?"

"I don't care. Show me around! I want to see everything!"

"I hoped you'd say lunch," he said, "but I guess we can make our way there gradually." He stuffed his hands into his pockets. "Mr. Dempster—he works the drug store counter most days—makes this chicken sandwich to die for, and I go at least once a week to have one, just to make sure he never stops having the stuff around to make it." George went on for several minutes, detailing the particulars of this Divine Sandwich, the secret of which was apparently thinly sliced pickled onion and dill mayonnaise dressing. I listened politely, wondering if food was an obsession to replace his obsession with pencil sketching of the previous year, or if he was merely expanding his interests. When at last he'd completed this Rhapsody on a Theme by Sandwichini, he turned to me. "So, why are you here? I mean, it's swell, but what happened?"

I told him about my intruded-upon room. "Mother's been too busy dashing about like a madwoman for me to have a chance to tell her about it, and she wouldn't tell me what spooked her into leaving. I did ask."

"Well, that shouldn't surprise you," he said sagely. "They never tell us anything."

He wasn't wrong. His own parents had been a fathomless well of secrets until I came along and began sniffing about, like a spaniel ready to flush out its prey. That's my curiosity for you. I'm not content with just letting things be, especially if it's someone else's business to which I am not personally attached. "Anyway, it's not fair they expect

14

us to tell them things when they never tell us things," I said.

For a few minutes we walked in silence, and I glanced over at George. He was still a couple inches shorter than I was (his pet peeve). He'd changed so much from that overalls-clad, barefoot boy I'd first met two years before. George wasn't flamboyant or vain like his father, but there was a new, tidy elegance to my friend that hadn't been there last summer.

And, of course, there were the new spectacles I hadn't yet seen in person. He'd written to me about them, of course. At his new school, he'd been given a seat in the back of the room, only to realize with dismay that he hadn't a prayer of reading the blackboard at such a distance. His teacher let him swap desks with a front-row student and sent home a note to George's parents, which led to a prompt appointment with one Dr O'Neill and a shiny new pair of specs. "I look like an owl," he'd complained, ending his letter with a drawing of an unimpressed owl in big round glasses.

"You look like your cousin Thomas, not an owl," I said. George was incredibly like his second-eldest cousin in many ways, except that instead of words and books and theology, Thomas' nose was always in a pile of fossils or bits of bone or things trapped in amber. "Anyway, I think they look very right on you."

"I just didn't want to get laughed at," he said. "Like what's-his-name in Turner. But he was the only one there, and lots of other kids have glasses here." He shrugged slightly.

"What's the school like here?" I asked.

"See for yourself," he said, gesturing dramatically as we turned a corner. "It's at the end of this block. Also, we get to cross Mill Creek between here and there! Just like going to school in Turner!"

I gaped as the huge building came into view: long, and white, and full of windows, with lots of open space all around. "That's... that's our school?"

"Aye right, miss," he drawled, parodying his father in one of his

Scottish Moods. "It's stupidly crowded though. There's a new school opening soon. Dad hopes I can go there next year instead. Either way, it'll be less crowded."

After a long time patiently waiting as I peered into one window after another, George informed me he was about to perish from starvation and would I please hurry up already.

I hurried.

His plaintive puppy eyes are very, very hard to resist.

At the drug store, the man behind the counter waved to George and beckoned us over to a couple empty stools near the end. I was surprised, when he opened his mouth, to hear a distinctly Scottish burr. "I'll have your sandwich in no time, George. Who's the young lass?"

George made the introductions and I agreed to try one of Mr. Dempster's Divine Sandwiches.

It was good.

I suggested it might be improved with the addition of some crunchy lettuce, and George feigned horror at this culinary blasphemy. We all laughed, and Mr. Dempster promised he'd add lettuce to mine next time. "For now," he said, "dessert. Did George talk this one up too?"

"Just the sandwich," I said, marveling at the giant dish of ice cream with two spoons stuck in that he placed before us. Mr. Dempster leaned his elbows on the counter and lowered his voice as if about to share state secrets. "Well, Louise, this lad has tried all my ice cream concoctions, but this is the one he always comes back to. It's called the Commodore Perry. You take a dipperful each of vanilla, French vanilla, and strawberry ice cream. Crushed strawberries go on the strawberry scoop, crushed pineapple on the vanilla, and grape juice on the French vanilla. Then a big dollop of whipped cream over it all, with glacé cherries tucked n. George usually eats the whole thing on his own, so don't wait too long to dig in." He winked and went to chat up some other customers, and I did dig in.

"It's amazing," I said, and we exchanged ecstatic ice cream faces. I managed to get most of my fair share before letting him polish it off.

"So is food your new fascination?" I asked, watching him lick

his spoon. He blinked at me as if the question confused him, set the spoon into the dish, and thought.

"I don't know," he said. "I guess I just like to eat."

He left the money on the counter and we went on down the street, east now, past the office of the law firm where Mr. Graham worked. We looked into the windows, even though it was closed and there was nothing to see.

"Wait 'til you meet Daisy Delight," George said as we turned homeward, eyes impish.

"Who's that?"

"Dad's secretary."

"That cannot be her real name."

"Of course it isn't!" He laughed, not protesting when I looped my arm through his, and went on. "Mamma told him if he hired anyone young and pretty, she'd build him a doghouse out back to live in. So he hired the oldest and ugliest applicant and gave her a pet name instead."

I giggled. "What'd your mother say about that?"

"Rolled her eyes. And then Dad said he'd always preferred older women anyway, so she swatted him with a tea towel and that was the end of it. They are *so* embarrassing."

"Is she older than he is?" I asked, surprised.

"Who, Mamma or Daisy?"

"Your mother, of course!"

"Yes. By two years."

"I'd never have guessed." Every married woman I knew was younger than her husband. My own mother was ten years younger than Daddy.

We passed the stately Capitol Building in amiable silence, then George pointed out the Presbyterian church. "It'll be nice to not go alone anymore," he said.

"Your dad never goes with you?"

George shook his head. "He stays home with Mamma, like he always has. He'll go with her to the services Rabbi Zylberman has at his house, but she only does that every few weeks."

George's parents fascinate me. Not only did Mr. Graham grow up in a plush and privileged existence in a Scottish castle, but Mrs. Graham is the daughter of a London rabbi. She refuses to divulge his name because, she says, he was cruel to her about her having a baby with someone else's husband, and she still has a grudge. I'm not sure quite what to think of that, because if I have a husband someday I wouldn't want him off having babies with someone else, either. George thinks she means that even if she'd been bad, she was still her father's daughter, and he should have loved her even if he didn't approve of what she did. I suppose that makes some sense.

(I wonder what I'd have to do to make my mother stop loving me. Because she does love me, even if she has an odd way of showing it.)

Anyway, whoever Mrs. Graham's parents are (were?), I think they must have been extremely strict, because Mrs. Graham says she is much less observant now than she was raised to be, and the way I see it, she still has an awful lot of rules she follows. About what she eats, and all the Friday night stuff, and the holidays. It all seems so exotic, and the fact that she and Mr. Graham, who is not Jewish, can peacefully exist under one roof is as odd and delightful to me as discovering Mrs. Graham is older than her husband.

Eventually we made our way back to the neighborhood of

Victorian houses where the Grahams lived. George stood at the foot of the front steps, staring up at the door and musing, "I wonder if they're done being secretive yet."

The house was enormous, at least ten times as big as The Dump (what we'd called the Grahams' house in Turner—a rickety, drafty, rundown mess of a place that barely held the three of them). This place needed a lot of love, but at least it wasn't literally falling apart.

It was just... so very *pink*.

Lavender would have been less atrocious.

And the paint was cracking and peeling like some sort of rare disease George probably could have found a name for. I said as much.

"It's an eyesore," he agreed. "But Mamma wants to get the inside fixed up first. She says that's the part *she* has to look at every day, and the neighbors can either be patient or come fix the outside themselves at their own expense."

I laughed, because I could hear her saying exactly that to anyone who came to express their complaints. George cast a glance back at the car. "Well, they've unloaded everything. Let's just poke our heads in and see."

He opened the door and listened for a moment. From somewhere I heard the adults' voices, and George said, "They're in the back. Come on."

I was simply dying to see what sort of room I'd have. We kicked our damp shoes off by the door and hung our hats and his coat on hooks in the entry hall. The place smelled cleanly of lemon and beeswax, a slightly incongruous scent for rooms that still looked so shabby and deserted, as if only inhabited by ghosts for the last fifty years.

"That's going to be the library," George said, pointing to the room on the left of the foyer. "And on this side, the sitting room. Not done, as you can see."

The bare floorboards were grey with age and neglect, but there was a couch and an armchair near the fireplace. "We don't use it much yet," George admitted. "Come upstairs."

That was the moment I fell irrevocably in love with that house: following him up that narrow, winding stair, walled with dark wood cleaned and polished to a sheen worthy of Uncle Jamie's Inverlochy

Castle, with a candle sconce in the center of each wooden panel. I paused to admire them. "Do you ever light these?" I asked, charmed beyond words.

"We haven't so far. Not honestly sure why Mamma decided to put them there. I'm the only one who goes upstairs much. Well, up to today, that is."

"It must look magical all lighted."

"Well, sometime we can light them. Hurry up!" he said, clearly immune to the charms of glowing flames along a staircase.

I trailed after him, fingers lovingly touching each sconce. At the top of the stairs, he threw open the door to our right. "This is yours. We had to improvise a bed. I hope it'll be all right."

"I don't mind that," I assured him, and I really didn't. I sat down on the neatly folded pile of blankets, covered with one of Mrs. Graham's quilts, and hugged my knees as I surveyed the room, spare and characterless and stripped of whatever wallpaper it once had.

"What this room needs is *pictures*," I said, reaching for my crate, which someone had kindly brought up while we were out. I unfolded my map fragments, which George helped me reassemble on the wall with lots of pins. Of course all my painstaking aviation-related location marking had come out and left lots of extra tears (no thanks to you, Anonymous Destroyer of Property), but I'd have to make do.

"School probably has an old map sitting around somewhere you could ask for," George said. He held up the pieces of Bessie Coleman to inspect them. "I think we could mount these others on stiff board and the tears would hardly show... who is this one, anyway?"

I drew Daddy's sweater closer around me and crossed my arms over my chest, surveying the map. "She's the first colored woman to get a pilot's license. She had to go to France to do it because white folks wouldn't let her here. Then last year she died when she fell out of a plane someone else was flying. She was thirty-four. Born the same year as my mother. I wish I could have met her."

George gave me a look which I knew meant All Pilots Are Lunatics and Why Would You Ever Want to Be One, but he had the sense not to say it out loud.

"She wasn't strapped in," I explained. "Trying to take pictures. *I* won't go up in the air not strapped in."

He shook his head slightly and changed the subject. "So what have you been doing all winter, then?" He dropped to the floor and lounged back so his head lay on the edge of my bed, and produced a box of crackerjacks from his pocket. He popped a piece into his mouth, then held the box out to me. I took one and laughed as I plunked down beside him.

"I took the car's engine apart."

"You didn't." But his dark eyes sparkled up at me.

"I did! And Mother nearly fainted when she found me outside surrounded by engine bits, but I put it all back together eventually, and then I taught myself to drive. Mother got the vapors over that, too, when Mr. Ball 'phoned to tell her I'd driven myself to his shop. She made him drive me back, but he said I'd done a good job. He better say that, since I spent so many hours asking him questions and watching him work until I had a pretty good idea what to do." I grinned and reached for another piece of crackerjack.

"Would you teach me how?" he asked.

"To take the engine apart?"

"No, daftie. To drive."

I laughed. "You'd need to sit on a cushion."

"I *will* be taller than you someday," he muttered.

"Oh, do stop harping on about that," I shot back. "All girls are taller than boys at our age."

"My manly egotism is still severely wounded," he replied with gravity, but I could tell he was trying not to laugh.

"Manly, my foot," I said. "Come back and tell me that when your voice drops and you have to shave."

His only response was to roll his eyes and pour the remaining crackerjack into his mouth, as if by quantity of consumption he could immediately spring up several inches, then proceeded to almost break a tooth on the metal fish charm he'd accidentally ingested. I couldn't stop laughing. I couldn't help it. It was just so *funny*. Fortunately he has a good sense of humor too and wasn't offended.

He gave me the fish, which I pocketed. "Show me the rest of the house?" I asked, scrambling to my feet.

He shoved the empty box back into his pocket and led me into the hall again, where he pointed to the furthest left-hand door. "That's your mother's room. But wait 'til you see mine. It's like having the entire Dump to myself!"

My mouth dropped open when, with a flourish, he threw open the door to his space. It wasn't only a bedroom; he had his own sitting room too!

I ran across to look out the window and see the back garden. He joined me. "I was only able to keep three of my hens," he said, pointing to the small coop in the corner of the lot. "Grapenut, Krumbles, and Pep. And only as long as they keep laying, Mamma says. Moo had to be sold, of course. I miss Sirius the most, though. Everything is so close here, and Mamma said—"

I anticipated the rest and turned on my best Imitation of Mrs. Graham Voice. "'We cannot justify the expense of keeping a horse that is no longer of legitimate use to us.'"

He burst out laughing. "In a nutshell, aye. It scares me how well you mimic her. Anyway, even without Sirius, it's pretty nice here. I think you'll like it too."

"What about Peach?" I asked. I already knew how Mrs. Graham had given his dog away, but I thought it was odd George didn't mention missing him, too.

"We don't talk about Peach," he said. Not angry, just resolutely quiet. I didn't push it.

"I don't care where I live, so long as the company's good," I said. "What about your parents? Where's their room?"

"Mamma's made them their own apartment downstairs, right under this room. She's hoping this can be a boarding house someday. If that ever happens, I'll get kicked out of here and have to use one of the smaller rooms, so I'm going to enjoy this as long as I can." He flopped backwards, arms outstretched, onto his bed.

I sat on the edge beside him but jumped straight back up again when I saw the phonograph. I am ashamed to admit this, but I SQUEALED.

"When did you get this? You never told me!!"

He sat up. "If I told you everything, my letters would be an inch thick. But Uncle Jamie sent it. At Christmas. It was for all of us, but I brought it up here a few days ago and just haven't taken it back down yet."

I reverently ran my fingers over it and flipped through his small collection of records. "Can I play one?"

"Of course."

I selected one at random, wound up the machine, and carefully set the arm down. The peppy tune set my feet tapping, and George laughed. "It's a foxtrot," he said. "Remember how to do that one?"

Last summer, at Inverlochy Castle, George's cousins taught us Scottish country dancing, and it was so fun that Aunt Estelle took George and handed me off to Vincent (her third son, the one who's unbelievably handsome as well as a bit mad), and they taught us to waltz and foxtrot.

"Of course I remember," I said. George came to move the arm back to the beginning and held out his hands to me and we swung off. It was a little stumbly at first, trying to match our rhythms to each other and the music properly, but eventually we worked it out, and then we danced through all his records.

"Just imagine if Uncle Jamie knew you were using his phonograph to play 'modern rubbish'," I giggled as we dropped onto his bed at the end.

"He already knows. I told him. He reproved me, but Aunt Estelle added a postscript saying 'pay no heed to my lord curmudgeon'."

"She adds postscripts to his letters to me, too, sometimes. She's so sweet and so funny."

"She's wonderful," he agreed.

When we were called down to supper, I hoped someone would call a family council, someone who was not Me, to explain what exactly had driven Mother and me so suddenly from our home.

But it didn't happen. We just sat and ate the delicious stew Mrs. Graham had made, and George detailed where all we had been and how amazing Mr. Dempster's sandwich was, at which point I tuned him out and watched Mrs. Graham as she moved between stove and table instead. I used to think she was passive and colorless, but after the family skeletons all came out and she and Mr. Graham got properly married, we were all surprised at just how much she can be a force to be reckoned with. Sometimes I wonder why my mother is friends with her, because they are so different. I know Mother is scandalized by Mrs. Graham's ability to curse like a sailor, not to mention the way she and Mr. Graham "carry on in front of everyone". I find both these things highly interesting and instructive, myself.

I guess opposites attract.

And also Mrs. Graham *did* practically save Mother's life at the end of 1925 when she got so sick right around Thanksgiving. Bullied her back from the brink of the grave, one might say.

At any rate, all the adults discussed during supper was what Mrs. Graham had planned for the upstairs bedrooms, and soon she and Mother were deeply engrossed in a boring conversation about wallpaper and carpets, while Mr. Graham lost himself in some heap of papers he'd brought home from his office.

After a nice bath, I climbed into my bed, pulled my quilt up to my chin, and snuggled into a ball around Clotilde. I wasn't sure why, but lately I'd felt a strong, if possibly babyish, urge to mother Clotilde, and found her presence very comforting.

At night.

When nobody could see me and make fun of me.

You see, Clotilde isn't really a doll. That is, she doesn't look like a *person*.

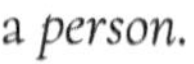

I wanted to learn to sew last summer when we were in Scotland, and in Aunt Estelle's scrap-bag was a piece of orange velvet leftover from a chair she'd recently had reupholstered. It was so soft and fun to pet, and I fell in love with it at once.

Vincent, who was lolling upside-down on his mother's nearby fainting couch, asked scornfully, "What can you make with that, a carrot?"

And I said it would make a fabulous giant carrot.

Aunt Estelle found some green wool to crochet her some leafy hair, and black buttons for her eyes, and I embroidered on a smile before Aunt Estelle showed me how to make neat, tidy hand stitches to shape and assemble the carrot. Then we stuffed her with fluff, and there's even a row of eleven tiny buttons and loops up her back so I can open her up and hide things inside, if I want to. Clotilde is a ridiculous, carrot-shaped, very huggable doll, and I would be awfully lonely in bed at night without her.

With my carroty-dolly-thing in my arms, and my repaired aviators watching over me from the walls, and the swinging foxtrot playing in my head, I closed my eyes and drifted off into contented sleep.

MARCH 6, 1927: SUNDAY

When I woke Sunday morning, it was to a light, relentless tapping on my door, and I remembered where I was and bounded up, dragging my quilt and Clotilde with me, because it was cold.

George was at my door, grinning. "I've already been out and delivered my papers, lazybones," he said. "Mamma's making waffles. Hurry up and get dressed!"

Mrs. Graham's waffles were not to be ignored. "I'll get dressed later," I said, reaching for Daddy's old sweater to put on over my nightgown, and pushed past him, running ahead of him down to the kitchen.

As I came in, Mr. Graham was finishing shaving at the mirror in their little sitting room off the kitchen. When I stayed with them for a few weeks in 1925, I'd gotten used to this unchanging routine he goes through, completely unflustered and undeterred by any of the chaos that might surround him. I do believe he'd shave even if some plague had struck the entire family down. It's a complicated procedure involving hot towels and steam and soap that he has down to a science. It takes him about a quarter of an hour.

This morning as he finished, I saw he'd added a new step: going over to Mrs. Graham for inspection (and, I think, fishing for a kiss or two). She sighed and said, "It's fine, George, it's always fine, you don't need me to look!" (Mr. Graham's name is also George. It's terribly confusing sometimes.)

Daddy didn't use a straight razor. It looks absolutely terrifying to me. But it's what Mr. G has always used, and he's just old-fashioned enough that he'll probably never change—the same way Uncle Jamie will probably still be using his antiquated pocket watch with its compass fob when it's 1959 and everyone else is using some other fancy time-telling gadget that hasn't been thought up yet.

Anyway, I also knew that before anyone else was up, Mrs. Graham would likewise have gone through her own morning routine, which entails Not Being Talked To Until She's Had Her Two Cups of Tea, as she has a long quiet sit with *Good Housekeeping* or that Jewish newspaper *Forverts* she gets sent from New York, her hair an uncombed frizz and her reading glasses sliding down her nose. This morning, she still hadn't combed her hair or gotten dressed when I arrived in the kitchen, but sometimes she goes all day without doing

either, so that didn't surprise me.

I said she is a force to be reckoned with, and she is, but George wrote to me that she still sometimes sits and stares into space as if she's not even on this planet. She used to be that way frequently, the year I met George, but she still does it here, just... not quite as often, I guess. Last summer when we went to Scotland, she and my mother stayed behind and basically lived together. We came home from Scotland to a Mrs. Graham who had chopped off her unkempt mane of hair into a bob and made herself an entirely new wardrobe to celebrate starting a brand-new chapter of her life in Salem. She said last summer with my mother was a Healing Time, but that she didn't know if she'd ever be 100% again.

28

As I found a chair, the sight and scent of the perfectly golden waffles, with their butter and syrup and whipped cream and summer-flavored peach sauce, made me realize just how hungry I was.

Mrs. Graham stood at the head of the table and spoke one of her Hebrew blessings. George, at its foot, repeated it in English. "Blessed are You, Lord our God, Ruler of the universe, who brings forth bread from the earth."

George then settled into his chair, his entire end of the table taken up with his plate on the left and the newspaper spread out on his right. I sat around the corner from him and watched as he mindlessly consumed EIGHT WAFFLES while scanning the news. Mr. Graham chattered about not much, the way he does. Mother quietly ate her waffle, while Mrs. G went back and forth between table and waffle iron, keeping us supplied.

She's the sort of person who is happiest when she is feeding people, and unlike my mother, she is an excellent cook. Mother can't manage to heat a can of soup without burning it, let alone create a tasty meal out of stray ingredients like Mrs. Graham can.

"What time does church begin here?" Mother asked.

"Sunday school at nine-thirty," George answered promptly without looking up. "Church at ten forty-five."

I smothered a laugh. Trust George to tune out everything until church was mentioned.

He vanished shortly afterwards and returned all suited up, hair pristine, but minus a tie. He saw my eyeroll as he slid back into his chair to resume reading the paper. "Why bother?" he said, with a small shrug.

"Considering he can't tie shoelaces either—" began Mr. Graham, only to be swatted on the shoulder with a tea towel by his passing wife and told to shush.

I sighed melodramatically and went up to the Helpless Boy's room. I knew from past experience that his belongings were always sorted and stored in a specific way, so I had no trouble locating his paltry selection of ties. I thought briefly of how different George was from his father, who liked his (dozens) of neckties to be as noisy as possible. George had three neckties, and two of them were black. I selected the one made from the Graham tartan and went back downstairs.

"Up," I commanded.

He reluctantly rose to his feet while I whipped that tie into a tidy knot, then straightened his collar and pushed him back into his seat. "*Now* you look civilized," I said. "Have you been going to school all year without a tie, too?"

"What do you think?" George asked. He blinked up at me, never looking more like that silly owl self-portrait, and went back to his paper.

At nine-twenty we set off for Sunday school, Mother and George and me. As George had predicted, Mr. Graham stayed home with his wife.

Despite having been born into a Presbyterian family and later switching to the Church of England to please his first wife's family, Mr. Graham is now a self-proclaimed member of the Church of Nothing Much.

"Didn't Mrs. Graham want you to be Jewish?" I'd asked him once.

"Not particularly," he'd said.

Secretly I suspected he and Mrs. Graham just really liked an opportunity to kiss each other without a peanut gallery.

George only became interested in religion two years ago when

> 1. Uncle Jamie, who is as devout as Mr. Graham is apathetic, started talking to George about God, and
> 2. George found out he's Jewish. The reason it took him so long to catch on was partly because his mother had had no spare energy to expend on his religious education after he was about four, and partly because he is, as I have said already, often unable to see the obvious.

Now George isn't merely 100% on board with believing in God, he also wants to be a minister when he grows up. Or a rabbi, I suppose? He's still working out exactly what he believes, which is a challenge when one's parents have two often opposing options to offer.

George really doesn't do anything halfway.

Always self-conscious of my poor reading skills, I asked George to leave me with the youngest children's Sunday school class, where I made myself useful to the teacher and charmed the little ones, which I am good at. It was far more fun than being shown up as a terrible reader to kids of my own age, who hadn't gotten to know me yet. George did introduce me to some of them afterwards, though, and they seemed pleasant enough.

After lunch, Mr. and Mrs. Graham went to their room to have a nap, and Mother went to hers for the same.

"Why do grownups always want to take naps?" I groused to George. "Such a waste of time! Napping! When you could be doing so many other things!"

He shrugged, flopped onto his bed, and started to reach for a book, but I said, "And you! Always reading!"

He blinked at me. "What have you in mind, then?" Before I could answer, he brightened and went on, "I could read you something! What do you want to hear?"

I liked that George didn't ask me if I still struggled with reading, didn't act as if I was a lesser being despite his being so far in advance of me there was no hope of my ever catching up. Books were hard for me: words on a page took hands and danced before my eyes, letters swapping places and jumping from line to line, so I stumbled a lot and got anxious, which made me stumble more. I could remember things just fine, if I heard them. Mimic any accent or learn lines for a school play in a snap if someone just helped me through them first.

Numbers were no trouble, but when I did try to read for pleasure, I was so busy trying to marshal the words into line that any coherence they held fluttered away in the meantime. I told George all that back in the early days of our friendship, when he got annoyed that books didn't hold the same magic for me that they did for him. I told him how, back at my first school in Junction City, I got taunted constantly for being so stupid, but my father used to read to me every night at bedtime, something just for me after we had our family Bible chapter together.

When George finally understood, he asked if he could read to me.

And I said yes.

He really is the sweetest boy.

George could pick up a book and give a cold performance better than I could have done reading through three times first. He liked to show off his talent for oration, and I supposed I shouldn't have been nurturing his already overgrown ego by encouraging it, but it really was the only way I could take in and enjoy a story.

I hopped on one foot over to his bookshelf, considerably more well-stocked than it had been in the old Dump days, thanks to his sisters sending him home last year with two boxes full of their old favorites that they weren't using anymore. He read me *Jane Eyre* on the trip home. But now I saw there were newer ones even than those,

and I slowly sounded out the unfamiliar titles. *Oliver Twist. Clouds of Witness. The Secret Adversary. Winnie-the-Pooh.*

That last seemed the least complicated of these options, so I pulled it off the shelf and brought it over. "Some of the kids at school talked about this one," I said. He grinned and took it from my hand.

I went to fetch my own pillow, and the two of us sat side by side on his bed, propped on our pillows against the headboard while George took me on a lovely journey to the Hundred Acre Wood. Despite his love of lofty, hefty classics, I could tell he was absolutely enjoying himself. I was particularly enamored of Eeyore, whom George voiced as a curmudgeonly Scotsman with a caber on his shoulder.

Two and a half hours later he shut the book with a snap, just like his dad does, startling me out of my dreamy haze to realize I'd been leaning my head on his shoulder. I blushed. Chances were he hadn't even noticed, but I wondered how long I'd been cuddling up to him like that and wanted to sink into the floor. A couple of years ago, even last summer, it wouldn't have mattered, but we weren't little kids anymore. At least I was conscious *I* wasn't. I scooched away from him a tiny bit and he slid down and closed his eyes.

"Guess I'll be an old person and take a nap now," he said solemnly, but a tiny quirk at the corner of his mouth betrayed him, and I swatted him with my pillow.

"Hey, watch my glasses," he said, ducking away.

"Feather pillows never hurt glasses! Take them off!" I said, raising the pillow again for another swipe. He rolled off the bed, taking his own pillow with him, and I chased him around the room, dodging his own well-aimed strikes, until the air was full of hovering feathers and we were both breathless and giggling on opposite sides of the room.

George can be almost human, sometimes.

"Why did we come here?" I asked at supper that night, since it had become obvious nobody planned to tell me.

Mr. Graham didn't miss a beat, didn't even look up from the soup he was ladling out. "Your mother's going to help Alice with the house."

I narrowed my eyes at him and his dismissive, breezy tone. "You can't fool me," I said. "Mother was scared. We left in a hurry. You really think I won't figure it out?"

"Louise!" Mother interrupted, shaking her head slightly. Her eyes said, *Don't.*

Mr. Graham met my gaze then over the suspended soup ladle. He knew I was nosy. It was my fault his wicked and bigamous self got exposed, after all—finding out that he'd never actually married George's mother because of that other wife still inconveniently alive in England. He had on his lawyer face now—completely, carefully blank—and he leveled it on me.

"How about," he said calmly, "you just trust us on this one?"

"If you won't tell me, I'll just find out another way."

"Louise," Mother said again, fidgeting with her napkin.

I ignored her. Mr. Graham stared at me an instant longer, and the matter was dropped.

They thought it was dropped, anyway. But they ought to have known me better than that.

MARCH 7–11, 1927:
MONDAY – FRIDAY

*I*t was a busy first week. On Monday, Mother went to school with us to register me, and after that it was a blur of new faces and the huge building to navigate. (My good sense of direction helped.) On her way back from school, Mother stopped at church and boldly requested to be put into the rotation for organ or piano playing, and to be given a key so she could come practice, since she'd had to leave her piano behind.

They granted her both.

So after that, when we went home from school, we could usually find her at the church, where she'd have already been practicing for hours. Often she'd be playing Daddy's favorite hymns (he was partial to Charles Wesley's) with tears streaming down her face, until she noticed us and pulled herself together. Poor Mother. She didn't get to properly grieve his death as long as Sam was around, I guess. Like Mrs. Graham, she's broken and has her own healing to do.

I just wish she'd let me share her grief instead of walling me out of it. It might be easier to reconcile ourselves to what happened if we could share it. Because I loved him too.

And I did meet Daisy Delight, because quite often George also stopped by the office after school, either to say hello or run errands for his father.

Daisy Delight is properly called Marguerite Addams, and I do believe she is completely made of steel, with her piercing grey eyes and severe grey hairstyle. She even stands as if she has a steel beam for a spine. George wasn't exaggerating about Mr. Graham flirting with her, either, albeit it in a harmless and hilarious kind of way, and

honestly I thought she seemed oddly fond of Mr. Graham despite—or because of?—his nonsense.

At school, I spent recesses with George, who hadn't really made any friends over the previous six months. He was used to being the Lonely Outsider, and didn't have a clue how to interact with people anyway. "What do you think about Dickens' use of anaphora in *A Tale of Two Cities*?" is not a line that will bring you instant friendships with the average twelve-year-old.

But I too knew what it was to be the Lonely Outsider. Just for different reasons. Back on the family farm in Junction City, I had nobody my age who liked me, and at school I was mocked mercilessly for not being able to read at all until I was nine, and still barely managing after that. At the family Sunday dinner gatherings, I was the butt of most jokes. Daddy started quietly taking us straight home after church, trying to protect me, but invariably some relative would come nosing in to find out why we hadn't joined the rest of the clan.

The Pearsons were inescapable and suffocating, a horde of blond-haired, blue-eyed supermen (in their own inflated opinions), full of hatred for anyone who wasn't Just Like Them (white and Protestant). They lumped me, and by extension my parents, into their People We Hate group. Daddy's evil cousin Sam was the one everyone looked up to with adoration.

Sam managed the farm with his sons Jim and Hank. His wife died ages ago, I don't know from what, but probably something like being beaten to death, slowly, over years. As far back as I can remember, Sam above everyone else in my weird extended family was a shadowy, spooky presence in my life.

And then my father died. Sam immediately married Mother and took her and me to Turner before we'd properly had time to realize Daddy was dead, let alone mourn him. Sam whisked us away from any possible hope of support or comfort to be even more isolated. We—Mother and I—were forced to pretend everything was peachy when we went to church, or when Mother attended or hosted sewing circles, or when I attended school, but we were scared. Always, always, scared, for reasons I'll eventually get to.

When I finally decided to talk to George for the first time, I knew I was taking a risk. Sam wouldn't want us to befriend or confide in anyone aside from him. But I was desperate, and I'd thought it through carefully and watched George for months before I approached him. I was tired of facing the world alone and wanted an ally, and I liked what I'd seen of George—liked his aura of seriousness and how incredibly smart he seemed.

That first day when I went to talk to him at the cemetery across the road from The Dump, I was terrified that he, like everyone else in my life, would scoff at me and reject me—but instead he casually recited the epitaph on a nearby gravestone (a totally normal way to start off a friendship, I know) and let me come home with him to bring in the cow.

Of course, it might have been the promise of getting to ride my bike that won him over at the time, but it wasn't long before we were friends, actual friends, for the first time in either of our lives. I'd had to be careful to keep George away from my house if I knew Sam would be home, but by the time Sam caught on to my self-preserving treachery, it was too late for him to stop the chain of events I'd set off.

"Do you mind not having lots of friends?" I asked George now, as we leaned our backs against the school wall, lunches on our knees, soaking up some weak spring sunshine.

"I have you."

It was so matter-of-fact. I glanced over at him, polishing off his lunch with the tenacious focus of a blow-fly. *Where DOES he put it all,* I wondered. I couldn't eat that much if I tried.

"You don't wish you had more boys as friends?"

He shrugged, licking crumbs off his fingers and casting a not-very-subtle look my way to see if I had any leftovers he could pilfer. "I fit in with the average boy even less than you do with the average girl. Why complicate what seems to be working just fine?"

He's smart and sweet, and I missed him so much during the months we were separated. It would have been so much more fun taking apart the car engine with him close by, reading to me while I blackened my hands and clothes with grease and oil and muck. I was about to relate this soppy sentiment when George spoke.

"Are you going to finish that sandwich?"

Yes, yes I was, thank you very much. "Nice to know where I stand in the grand scheme of things," I murmured, taking another bite.

I hoped for several days, even after Mr. Graham's evasive answer, that the subject of why we were here would come up again and I'd get a more satisfactory answer. But no such luck.

My stepfather, Sam, worked so hard to keep us constantly terrified. I don't know if Mother and I will ever be able to talk freely about anything that happened with him, ever. Not that we really did before either. Sam might be dead, but the fear he planted in us is thriving like a weed. I guess that's what's holding me back from pushing harder for an answer.

Life is full of contrasts, though. When things were darkest with Sam, there was Uncle Jamie.

I met him in 1925 when he accompanied George's eldest sister Susan to Oregon for a Rather Confrontational Surprise Visit. (That was my doing, although in my defense it did not play out as I had imagined, and I feel very lucky that it all was okay in the end.) Uncle Jamie has a long string of names, but his wife calls him Jamie and that stuck. He's musical—sings and plays piano and flute beautifully. He was an army captain in the Great War, where he lost a foot after someone shot it and infection set in.

But those are all just stark facts that could be easily be about lots of men. What makes Uncle Jamie special, the reason he's become so important to me, is how *kind* he is, how he is never too busy to listen if you need to talk to someone. He took notice of me that summer, when I desperately needed the notice of a responsible, impartial adult. In my head, I like imagining he's my father, now that my own is dead. And he doesn't mind my calling him Uncle Jamie, even though he's not really. It makes me feel like I'm no longer completely alone, knowing that he has a great lively family who have all taken me in as if I belong.

I found out last summer that he has a habit of rescuing girls like me, girls who have dangerous fathers or other relatives. Of course *he* never mentioned it; I had to figure it out on my own. He and Aunt Estelle give them a safe place to be. I made friends with the current bunch of these girls last year. They live in a house of their own that's tucked away in the castle gardens, under the care of a motherly old lady, although they're welcome in the castle anytime they want to be there. Those girls proved to me that there are other people who really do understand what it's like to live with scary people who do horrible things.

MARCH 12, 1927: SATURDAY

*T*he first Saturday after we came to Salem, I decided I wanted to learn to make cookies to sell to the neighbors, to earn money for my paltry airplane fund. If the Girl Scouts could do it, why not me?

(I will tell you a secret right now. They can do it because someone else makes their cookies for them.)

Mrs. Graham was out with Mother doing some shopping, and I knew she wouldn't mind my using the kitchen as long as I cleaned up after myself. I opened the nearest not-Yiddish newspaper to the recipe section and selected the easiest-looking recipe. If it flopped, this past week with George had taught me he could be depended upon to annihilate all but the worst failed experiments.

As if some inaudible signal had beckoned him, George materialized at my elbow the moment I took a mixing bowl out of the cupboard.

"If you're going to hover," I said, "you can jolly well help out." I pushed a packet of dates in his direction. "It says to slice a cup of those."

"Okay," he said. "A cup before they're sliced or after?"

"How should I know? Does it matter?"

"Well, it'll be fruitier if you slice first and measure after."

"After, then."

He selected a knife and poured the dates onto the cutting board. "How thin?"

"It doesn't say. It just says slice them."

"How thin do you want them sliced?"

I waved him off in despair. "How about an eighth of an inch? Any more questions?"

"No," he said, unperturbed, and hummed quietly to himself as he began to slice those dates. I turned on the oven and sifted the flour, and beat the eggs and sugar. When George had scraped his one cup of disturbingly uniform date slices into the flour bowl, I asked what kind of nuts we had.

He scratched his head. "We had peanuts," he said.

"But you ate them."

"I might have." (He definitely had.) Then he brightened. "Walnuts from the neighbor! Only they're not shelled."

"Well, shell some then."

He obediently departed and I soon heard him out on the back porch hammering energetically.

He returned with the required quantity of nuts, plus a handful of extra ones he was munching on. I snitched one and popped it into my own mouth, chopping the rest into teensy bits. It was hard to do it the way Mrs. Graham did; her hands worked with fluid certainty, swift little chop-chop-chops that hardly seemed to move and yet left a small pile of nut bits behind. I couldn't crack eggs one-handed like she did either.

Yet.

Finally I stirred everything together while George oiled a pan for me. "This looks awfully dry," I said, staring at the contents of the bowl.

He came to look. "Add a little water, maybe?"

"Maybe." I added a few tablespoonsful to the mixture and tried to work it in with my fingers. It became very gooey where the water hit, and dry as sand everywhere else. But at last I managed to get it somewhat mixed, and I pressed the mess into the pan and slid it in to bake.

We stood there, staring at the oven and the clock in turns. When the pan came out, its contents were as flat as a fresh tarmac.

"They taste better than a fresh tarmac," George offered. "Marginally." I just glared with my arms crossed, and then our mothers walked in.

George explained the situation, ending with the pronouncement: "Basic survival biscuits."

Mrs. Graham laughed and took a bite of one—a difficult task

without breaking one's teeth—and agreed with him.

I showed her the recipe and she shook her head. "These proportions are preposterous! They shouldn't have you put in so much flour at the start, for one thing. Even three cups sounds excessive. That's always dead last, or should be. How much did you use?"

"All four cups," I sighed.

"Well, next time start off with two and a half."

It was kind of her to assume there would be a next time. "I'm not trying it again. These are rubbish."

"They're certainly not going to stay 'fresh and moist indefinitely'," Mrs. Graham murmured. George gathered the Basic Survival Biscuits into a tin and held it close to himself as he sidestepped out of the kitchen. I didn't protest. If he wanted to eat food scraps like one of his precious chickens, I wouldn't stop him.

"What is wrong with him?" I asked nobody in particular. "You'd think he was in the middle of the desert and wasting away."

Both mothers laughed, and Mrs. Graham said, "He's twelve," as if that explained anything.

After I washed up the cooking things, I went out back and George's hens came clucking over to see if I came bearing treats. Could even they think of nothing but food? I held out the piece of B. S. B. I'd stuck in my pocket earlier and Krumbles politely pecked at it once, then

flapped as if mortally offended by the offering and led her two minions off in search of bugs.

"I guess I'll have to think of some other way to make money besides selling cookies," I said upon re-entering the house, and flopped onto a kitchen chair. Mother was putting away the groceries while Mrs. Graham prepared a chicken for roasting, and they both turned towards me. Mrs. Graham looked thoughtful.

"You're good with children," she said at last. "Ask your church ladies to bring their little ones here for you to look after when they need to go out."

It was a brilliant idea, and my gloom evaporated instantly. Entertaining children would be much easier and more fun than trying to bake things. I gave Mrs. Graham a grin and a hug, forgetting until afterwards that she's not very fond of people touching her, and ran upstairs to ask George for help making a poster to hang up on the church notice board.

I found him in his room, consuming the Basic Survival Biscuits at a rate that would have brought disillusionment to his adoring and culinarily discriminating hens. I flopped onto the bed beside him and cocked my head to see what he was reading.

Hebrew. Of course. Rabbi Zylberman's latest assignment, probably. "Shouldn't you be working on your arithmetic?" I asked him.

"I should be," he said, around a mouthful of Basic Survival Biscuit, "but that would be worse than these edible paving stones."

"You don't *have* to eat them," I pointed out. "Even your chickens turned up their beaks. Come on, I'll help you. And then you can return the favor and make me a poster."

He heaved a huge sigh, closed his book, picked up another vile B. S. B., and fixed me with the expression of an affronted puppy whose sore paw has just been trodden on. He is very good at this expression, and it might work with his father, but I am immune.

"You did say you wanted to jump ahead a grade so you can finish school early," I reminded him. "You'll have to improve your grades in arithmetic if you really want to do that."

He reached down to his bookbag on the floor by his bed. He

44

pulled out his math book and a composition book and a pencil, and in a few minutes he and I were sitting cross-legged on the bed with the books in front of us and I proceeded to nicely bully him through his fractions and percentages, drawing him pies and cakes and Basic Survival Biscuits to drive the lessons home.

It did baffle me that something as straightforward as numbers could confuse anybody. 30 - 12÷3×2 is always going to come out 22. I suppose he was as baffled that I couldn't enjoy reading, but consider the fact that there are at least seven ways to pronounce O-U-G-H, and not one of them is OWG.

List of Stupid Words

Thorough : oh

Enough : uff

Cough : off

Hiccough : Up

Through : oo

Thought : aw

Plough : ow

MARCH 13, 1927: SUNDAY

*W*e had an argument at the breakfast table this morning, and it has left me rather upset.

Thea Rasche started it. (Mr. Graham says it's pronounced *Tay-a Rah-shah*.) She's a German aviatrix and there was a piece in the paper about her and this is what it said:

> *I know of no more stimulating feeling than that of soaring high above everything mundane. It gives me a feeling of freedom, of being detached from the things of earth that is simply indescribable.*

I *know* Mother doesn't want me flying; she gets very frantic when I talk about my plans to be a pilot. So I mostly only talk to George about it. But I was so excited to see a story like that one, about a woman pilot, quoting her as expressing a feeling I've always been able to imagine so strongly. I think it must be like going very high on a swing, except more so. Anyway, I had George read it to me, right there, unwilling to wait. After he finished, I said I understood Miss Rasche's struggle with her father, who is also unimpressed with the idea of a girl flyer. Mother got all tense, and George went off on a tangent *again* about how many stories there are each week about pilots crashing and dying, and I said automobiles kill far more people than airplanes, and—all right, I *didn't* need to call George what I called him, as it also reflected rather badly on his mother, who was not involved in the discussion at all—but it felt like a betrayal that he wouldn't stick up for me, and Mother began to cry, and I stalked out.

So we went to church in rather strained silence, George minus a tie, and me charging ahead so I didn't have to talk to him or Mother. I hid myself away with the little kids' class again, which reminded me I forgot to bring along my poster for the board, which made me even grumpier.

So by the time we got home, instead of joining the others for lunch, I locked myself into my room and sulked alone while I started a letter.

> *Dear Uncle Jamie,*
>
> *I hope you are having a better day than I am having. Everyone is mad at me for wanting to fly! As if I don't know there's danger involved! Anything can kill you in the right circumstances!! We all got into a flap at breakfast about it and I called George a—well, I won't write what I called him, I AM sorry about that—I just wish they'd understand that I'm not stupid and I want this more than ANYTHING I ever wanted before and I won't "grow out of it", as if I'm five and being dismissed with a pat on the head for saying I will be a fairy when I grow up or something! I bet you knew already when you were twelve what you wanted, didn't you?*

I was interrupted just then by a knock on the door. "Who is it?" I asked, suspicious, closing the book.

"Alice."

(Mrs. Graham is always telling me to call her Alice. I just can't.)

I got up to let her in, a little surprised that she was the adult coming to talk to me. She closed the door after herself and sat beside me on my bed, drawing her knees up and resting her chin on them.

"Did Mother send you?" I asked.

"No," she said. After a minute she turned her face towards me. "Where did you hear that—thing you called George?"

"You," I said, before thinking, then bit my lip.

But she laughed. "I have a rather foul mouth at times, I'm afraid," she admitted. "You know, once upon a time I was as timid and retiring as your mother, Louise? Goodness knows what George's father ever saw in me. I wouldn't have ever dreamed, up until meeting him, and

even for a long time after that, that I could ever become such a wanton hussy."

"But you're not," I said.

"Appearances can be deceiving," she replied briskly. "George's father taught me all those words. Thought it was funny to hear them out of Mousy Little Alice. And I loved to make him laugh—anyway, don't be like me, all right?"

Mrs. Graham's voice is beautiful; I love her accent and how even her tone always is. She looked out the window for some time, and we were both quiet. I waited, wondering where this was going.

At last she spoke. "I wanted to do more than just raise roses. I love my roses, mind. But I wanted more. I thought when I married my first husband, I'd have some excitement and adventure, but it turned out I didn't get much of either. He was kind, but he was always sort of standoffish, not how I thought a husband would be. I worried maybe I wasn't good enough for him or something. And I was scared when he died, shocked that it was so sudden, but not really sad. It felt surprisingly good to have a house of my own and a life of my own where nobody was instructing me what to do all the time."

"Why are you telling me this?" I asked, although I was drinking it up, and I think she knew it. She doesn't talk very much about things that happened long ago.

"I—I just want you to know that I understand about the aeroplanes. I think I understand why it appeals to you. Freedom, perhaps? Independence?"

My mouth dropped open. "Yes," I said. "That's it exactly."

She nodded, picking bits of lint off her navy wool skirt. "I hate to give my parents any credit after how they treated me, but I think they did care, albeit in their own misguided way. And your mother's just afraid of losing you. You're all she has left. She's not trying to be unkind, I promise you."

"I guess," I answered. Tears unexpectedly stung my eyes, but I blinked them back.

"Give her a few years to get used to the idea, and perhaps she'll come 'round to it." Mrs. Graham stood, and as she turned the doorknob, I looked up, startled.

"Aren't you going to make me come down and apologize?" It was what my mother would have demanded.

She smiled faintly. "That is for you to decide to do on your own time and conviction." And then she was gone.

Well, if I hadn't felt guilty about it before, I certainly did now, thank you, Mrs. Graham.

That night, still having managed to avoid my mother all day, I heard her cross the floor to my bed. I knew her step by its delicate, almost silent-ness, and I pretended to be asleep, keeping my eyelashes down as she dropped to her knees to see if I was awake.

She sighed, almost as if disappointed, and bent down to lightly kiss my cheek. And she whispered something very strange, in a voice that sounded stuffy from tears.

"Stay angry, little one. You're going to need it."

Then she left, and for a while, I was wide awake wondering why she waited until she thought I was sleeping to show me any affection, and what her odd words meant. Why would she want me to stay angry, when it was her who made me that way in the first place?

MARCH 14, 1927: MONDAY

*T*oday things seemed to have blown over, back to normal, and after school I stopped in at church to put up the poster George had helped me make. It wasn't very big, but it was colorful, and I was confident it would catch some mothers' eyes.

After that we went to the library, and on our way back (with half a dozen books that George would have consumed long before they were due), we passed a building so boring it caught my eye for boringness amongst the surrounding prettier buildings. "What's that?" I asked him, shifting my load of five books from one arm to the other.

He looked up from the sixth book open in his own hands and seemed to be disoriented for seconds before answering. "It's the Crystal Gardens ballroom. They have dancing a couple nights a week."

"Oooh, we should go sometime," I said, hugging my pointy-cornered burden close in an attempt to contain my excitement as I ran up to try the door.

To my surprise, it was unlocked, and I walked in, followed slowly by George, who was reading again.

There was a board near the entrance and I studied it in the dim light, then reached for George's arm and dragged him closer. "Look!" I said in a hushed squeal. "Ballet lessons!"

"It's French," he said. "Ball-*ay*, not ball-*et*."

"Whatever," I said. "Would you do it with me?"

He gave me a Look, but closed his book with a sigh to read the poster, humoring me, expression contemplative.

"Learn the centuries-old art of ballet," the poster said, above a picture of some elegant dancers in gorgeous costumes. "Taught by Tabitha Wisniewski, former principal dancer in the Ballet of the

Polish National Opera. Boys and girls of all ages and experience levels welcome." The poster had a little paper pocket beside it full of cards with Mrs. Wisniewski's name and telephone number.

"Do you really think my penny-pinching mother is going to spring for ballet lessons?" George said.

"She's only that way out of habit. I bet she'd say yes."

His expression had changed as he read the poster, and I could tell

he really wanted to do it. He loved dancing, possibly even more than I did. But he was balancing his inclination against the reality that he'd probably be bullied if he did say yes and boys at school found out. Despite not having any real friends besides me, I understood how hard it would be to do something so riskily *other* when you're twelve, because it's an age of extremes. Other kids will be either extremely nice or extremely mean. There's not a lot of in-between, and unlike me, George wasn't used to being kicked around. Faced with conflict, he tended to shrink into himself. Like that time I had to punch a classmate back in Turner for insulting George, because George was just sitting there like a deer in headlights.

He turned and walked out of the building, still silent. I took one of the cards from beside the poster and hurried after him. He was so lost in thought I was able to offload his own books back on him and he didn't even notice. We were almost home before he spoke.

"I read about ballet in the encyclopedia at school once," he said, pausing to lean against a tree. "I had just finished a book about Tchaikovsky. He wrote a lot of ballets and I didn't know what it was. It's not common over here, but it's a really big deal in Russia and eastern Europe. If that woman was a principal dancer in Poland, she must be really good." His eyes were lost in some far-off world.

"Does that mean you'll do it?" I asked.

He came back into my world and looked up at me. "On two conditions."

"Which are?"

He started walking again. "That Mamma agrees without an argument."

I sighed, feeling that this mission was already doomed under that condition. "Okay, what's the other?"

"You keep your mouth shut about it at school."

"Well, *that* goes without saying," I said, almost insulted that he'd doubt my dedication to protecting him.

We were both in for a surprise when I brought it up that evening, cozily congregated in George's parents' sitting room. Mother was knitting, Mr. Graham was making notes about some case he was working on, and Mrs. Graham was marking up George's latest Hebrew assignment from Rabbi Zylberman with an unapologetic red pencil. I took a deep breath and pulled out Tabitha Wisniewski's card and held it out to Mother.

"I want to take ballet lessons," I said.

She looked up from her knitting with surprise, but not bad surprise. I read a sort of relief in her expression, as if she'd despaired of me ever wanting to do anything Refined and Ladylike. She took the card and studied it. "I think that sounds marvelous," she said, handing the card to Mrs. Graham. "Don't you think so, Alice?"

Mrs. G gave a cursory glance at the card and passed it on to her husband as I dropped the crucial bit of information. "But I only want to do it if George does it with me."

Mr. and Mrs. Graham looked up as one and fixed their eyes on George. Mr. Graham set down his pen and said, "Do you want to, son?"

There was no hesitation. "Yes," George said.

"I guess that's that, then." He tucked the card into his waistcoat pocket and Mrs. Graham, uncommonly serene about the whole thing, didn't raise any objections. He made all the arrangements first thing the next day. We'd go Mondays, Tuesdays, and Thursdays after school, starting that very night.

MARCH 15–27, 1927: TUESDAY – SUNDAY

*O*ur teacher told us to call her Mrs. Tabitha, "because nobody can pronounce Wisniewski". (I proved she was wrong and at least one person could. It means cherry tree, which I think is simply lovely.)

She also happens to be Jewish, which gave her an immediate bond with George. (She's only lived here for two weeks, which is why their paths hadn't crossed yet.) He told her how to get in touch with Rabbi Zylberman and invited her to dinner on Friday, too.

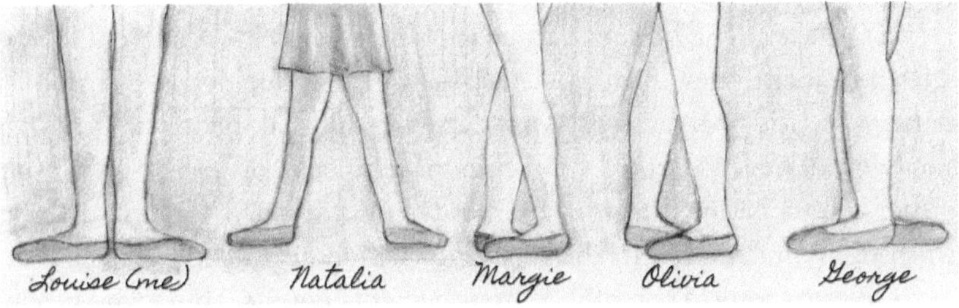

For an hour and a half we were drilled on seemingly inconsequential things, like stretching and positioning our feet five different and very specific ways. I bet George loved that. He is the only boy in the class, and the four other girls seemed delighted by his presence. Two of them, Olivia and Natalia, are Mrs. Tabitha's daughters, and Olivia has been doing this for a while already, but she was very helpful to the three of us who were completely new to all of it. Natalia is a chubby, adorable five-year-old. Olivia is eleven and says she's seen me around school. I liked both of them at once. The other girl is eight and her name is Margie.

(Margie's first words to me were, "Why are you wearing your long underwear to dance in?"

"Because if I take them off I turn into a dragon," I said.

I think she actually believed me.)

"We have to go up to a school in Portland when it's time for us to begin partnering," Olivia said. "There are more boys there. This is just a tiny school."

"It is tiny because it is new," Mrs. Tabitha said. "It will become more."

I woke up on Wednesday aching in places I didn't know could ache, and I was glad I could have a night off before returning on Thursday for more. But George said we would get used to it soon enough. (He proved to be right, as I think he would want me to add here.)

At any rate, I welcomed the day off that first week. The reason Mr. Graham arranged the days he did for us was because George had a standing arrangement with Rabbi Zylberman on Wednesday nights that was part of a bargain he'd made with his mother.

At the end of his visit in 1925, Uncle Jamie presented George with a beautiful new Bible, because George had decided he wanted to believe in God. Afterwards, Mrs. Graham told George that, although she would never dictate his religious choices for him, she wasn't either about to let him join a Christian church without first being thoroughly instructed in the faith into which he'd been born.

George couldn't really remember, of course, but for nearly the first five years of his life, his mother had still been a devoutly observant Jew, and he'd gone to synagogue and kept Sabbath and all the feasts and stuff. There are a lot more Jewish people in New York State than there are here, so it was easy for her to do. But then something happened, which even I have not been able to figure out, and after that the only remnant of her Jewishness was how she ate. It's only been in the last year that she's really begun easing back into her former ways, and I think it's largely for George's benefit. She feels just awful that she let things slide.

Mrs. Graham says if your mother is Jewish, you are, like it or not. The Jewish community in Salem is small—far too small to have a proper synagogue—but still Mrs. Graham managed to ferret out Rabbi Zylberman, who was over seventy and had come here from somewhere in the midwest to join his children. George, dutiful and sometimes nauseatingly perfect son that he is, submitted to a year of in-depth instruction in Judaism before making his choice.

Unsurprisingly, George *adored* studying Hebrew and excelled at it, hounding his mother for further instruction at home in between his sessions with the rabbi. He also got her to speak Yiddish with him, which he once upon a time knew better than English, but forgot it after they came to Oregon, and he wanted to learn it again. (I tried to pick it up as much as possible too, since I was dying to know what exactly Mrs. G and Rabbi Z were saying when they got into their verbal sparring sessions.)

George discussed everything he learned with both Uncle Jamie and Reverend Tully from our Salem church, digesting both sides of every argument and thriving on it all.

Typical George.

He went on studying even after his year was up, and every other week Rabbi Zylberman would come over on Friday nights for the welcome-in-Sabbath meal. Sometimes his children and grandchildren came too, but it usually was just him.

He wasn't what I expected, the first time I saw him. I guess somehow I got tainted by what George called "antisemitic stereotypes" without knowing it. I'd pictured a long, unkempt beard and shifty eyes and black robes. I'm ashamed to admit that here, now. But since I already got told off by George, I might as well put it down for the record and say I was so very wrong.

Rabbi Zylberman had no beard at all and wore an ordinary suit that was blue, not black. His eyes are bright and cheerful and he has a peppery personality that brings out Mrs. Graham's own pepper. They argue a lot, often lapsing into Yiddish, but it's not angry fighting, if that makes sense. Mrs. Graham says Jews are excellent arguers and thrive on debate, and there is no way some secret Jewish cabal is plotting world domination because "we can't even agree on whether sour cream or applesauce is the correct latke topping; how could we

POSSIBLY coordinate anything large and menacing? You stuff that into your Klan cousins' pipes and make them smoke it!"

(She knows my relatives have talked far too much about this in my hearing, and it was nice to be assured they were wrong.)

So between the rabbi, school, his paper route, and now dance lessons, George had plenty to keep him occupied all day, every day.

I did not.

I hoped I'd soon have mothers responding to my poster on the church board. If they didn't, I'd have to plot a more aggressive campaign of going door to door advertising my services.

But then the notes started coming.

MARCH 28, 1927: MONDAY

I came into the girls' changing room at dance class and found, to my relief, that the bag I forgot to bring home Thursday was still there. I dug through it to make sure nothing was missing, and a piece of card caught my eye.

I was sure it wasn't mine, but I picked it up, thinking perhaps it was someone else's and got put into my bag by mistake.

Almost before I fully read it, I crushed it in my hand and threw it to the floor, glancing around furtively. I was the first one here. Anyone could have come in over the last three days and done this.

I changed quickly, stuffing the paper deep into my bag just as Olivia and Natalia walked in. All through class, I felt jittery and cold and distracted, and the exacting Mrs. Tabitha had to snap at me several times to get me to pay attention.

"What's eating you?" George asked as we left the building afterwards. Unlike me, he was quite pleased with life just then. Mrs. Tabitha had almost praised him twice tonight, which meant he was either doing very well or he was becoming her favorite as the only boy.

I rifled in my bag 'til I found the note and shoved it at him. "Who did this?"

He blinked at me, took the note, inspected it, and stopped walking so he could stare off into space for a moment.

Feeling a bit braver with George holding it, I looked at it again myself. It was a simple message beside a crudely drawn grim reaper holding a scythe.

I sat down on the curb and hid my face in my knees.

"Hey," George said gently, sitting beside me and trying to look into my face.

"It's Daddy's scythe," I whispered, muffled, into my skirt.

"Why his in particular? Isn't a scythe a scythe?"

I sat up. "His had his initials woodburned into the handle. See, that's what that's supposed to be by the blade," I said, pointing to a tiny *L. P.* in the drawing.

My mind spun back to that hot summer morning, the morning I saw my father die.

Hand in hand I went to the hayfield with Daddy, as I'd done

dozens of times before, trailing after him at a safe distance as he expertly swung his blade, leaving a swath of sweet-scented felled stalks to our left. I heard a voice call out, saw Daddy stop to look for the source of the voice, saw him lower his scythe. Something struck his ankles; the scythe dropped from his grip and he fell forward. I saw him fall onto his scythe, saw the blade go into his chest silver and come out of his back red.

I ran to him. He managed to turn his face to mine and force out words in a hoarse, breathless voice so unlike his usual one. "Sam. Don't trust him. Take care—take care of your mother, because—"

I'll never know what that "because" was leading to. His mouth became too full of blood to speak anymore, leaking out all over my hands holding his face. Before he even had time to choke on it, his eyes drifted closed, and that was that.

I clapped my bloody hands over my mouth in horrified panic, the sharp metallic smell assaulting my nose. I thought I might be sick from the suddenness of it all, when my eyes caught sight of Sam, ambling in our direction with a slingshot sticking out of his back pocket. And I met his eyes, the cold blue Pearson eyes I've often wished I hadn't inherited, and I screamed at him, "You killed him!"

Sam's trademark smirk played about his mouth as he crouched down on the other side of my dead father, my only shield the murderous blade between his shoulders, and I scooted backwards, away from Sam's evil presence, stumbled to my feet, ran like the wind to my mother. I knew he was following me, but I still got to her first.

When Sam caught up, he came into the house without knocking and grabbed me roughly by my bloody wrists, tossing me outside, locking the door.

He shouldn't be alone with my mother. That was my first thought. I pressed my ear to the door. I heard him say she'd be next if she didn't obey him. Heard him slap her, hard, and her shoes scraping against the floor as she staggered backwards.

I never understood hate until that moment.

Meanness was Sam's game. We'd always known it. Daddy was the only one in the entire Pearson clan who actively and openly disapproved of Sam, who in his turn was equally active and open about his hatred for my parents and me, lumping us in with Jews and blacks and Catholics.

I was nine. I knew about that other Klan, the one with a K, and I knew most if not all of my male Pearson relatives were in it. They were men who talked big and acted little. I certainly never imagined that even Sam would actually murder someone. You're naïve like that when you're little. You hear about bad things, but you don't really believe they're real.

Until your beloved father bleeds to death in a lonely hayfield and there is nothing you will ever be able to do to bring him back.

Only Mother and I, and George and Uncle Jamie, know the whole truth about how my father died. That Sam killed him.

Or... we *thought* we were the only ones, now that Sam himself is dead.

The note, the crudely drawn grim reaper, with my father's scythe, and the brief message in block letters.

LYDIA'S TURN IS COMING.

I couldn't help myself. I was sick right into the street. George rested a light hand on my shoulder, waiting patiently for me to stop panicking. It felt like ages. But maybe it wasn't. And then, his hand still on my shoulder all the way, he got me home.

I went straight up to my room, hiding the note deep in Clotilde's stuffing so my mother would never find it. Inside my cuddly carrot, it no longer seemed like such a threat. I could pretend it didn't exist.

Mother came fluttering in soon after. "George says you were sick on the way home!"

I nodded, closing my eyes and resting my head on Clotilde. "I don't want to eat supper."

She knelt down and laid the back of her hand on my forehead. I wished she'd leave it there, or go on to stroke my hair, or climb into bed beside me and hold me. But she didn't do any of those things. "George has gone to fetch some ginger beer," she said. "Perhaps that will help."

Nothing can help, I thought. But I thanked her in a whisper, and she left me alone with a promise to come check on me again soon.

A little while later, George came in, his pillow hugged under one arm and the bottle in his other hand. I sat up, arranging my pillow behind me, and took a tentative sip. I didn't love ginger beer, but at least drinking it gave me a sense of control, an illusion of being able to do something about my troubles. George lounged back against his own pillow beside me. "Where'd you put it?"

I didn't have to ask what "it" was. "Clotilde ate it."

He nodded, as if it was a completely normal thing to hide poison pen letters inside a stuffed carrot.

"It's strange," he mused. "None of the Wisniewskis have any way of knowing any of these details, and Margie's not in our school. Who else possibly would?"

"Sam," I said.

"He's dead."

"I know." There was a long pause. "You won't tell Mother, will you? About the note?"

"Why would I? Anyway, I think she already knows something's up. Why else would you have come here so suddenly? And she's not trying to find work or a place of your own to live. Maybe that's because she doesn't want to be alone and this is her safest option. The redecoration is just an excuse."

Occasionally—very, very occasionally—George displays shocking levels of astuteness in practical everyday matters. I studied his profile, silhouetted against the grey almost-evening light from my curtainless window, and as if struck by lightning, I had a vision of the incredibly gorgeous person George would grow up to be, and something inside me fluttered—instantly snuffed out by remembering what an unattractive stick I was in comparison.

What in the world is wrong with you, Louise? I scolded myself. *You're nowhere near grown up enough to be in love with anyone. And you sure as heck don't deserve George.* I turned my face away from him, focusing instead on the ginger beer bottle, and I punished myself for my stupidity by taking a giant gingery swig that made me cough.

George sat up to see if I required intervention. I didn't.

"Want me to stay in here tonight?"

I nodded.

"Okay. I'm going downstairs for a bit. You may not want dinner, but I'm starving." (Of course he was.) "I'll be back."

I finished off the bottle, changed into my nightgown, and brushed my teeth. Exhausted from the day's drama, I was asleep before he came back, but I knew he had been there because the next morning his quilt and pillow were spread a few feet from mine when Mother came in to see if I was well enough to go to school. I told her I was, because sitting in bed brooding all day was the last thing I needed.

I only picked at breakfast, and when lunchtime came at school I had no appetite for that, either, so I gave it to George, who did. I watched him consume the double portion of sandwiches, bananas, cookies, and potato salad with detached awe. All I could think of with any clarity was that my mother was in danger and I mustn't let her be hurt.

Still, by the end of the school day, the grinding edge of my anxiety had dulled just enough that I began to regret the selfless sacrifice of my lunch, and my head ached.

I did only marginally better at our dance lesson that night than the previous night, but this time it was because I was realizing how hungry I was, and by the time the lesson ended, I was unbelievably grouchy.

But I was startled out of my grouchiness upon our arrival home by the sound of piano music coming from the sitting room. We poked our heads in and Mother was sitting at her piano—her own, actual piano!—with tears streaming down her cheeks. She saw us and fished out a handkerchief to wipe her face clean, but her eyes were bright and shining, not sad. I sat on the bench beside her, and she whispered, "Mr. Graham arranged to have it brought from the house as a surprise."

I've already mentioned how hesitant Mother is about physical affection. Not in the same way as Mrs. Graham, who actively dislikes people touching her if they aren't Mr. Graham. As far back as I can remember, it's always felt like Mother's holding back, that she'd *like* to hug me, but she's afraid to for some reason. Daddy was a little detached that way too. I never questioned their love for me, but there just weren't hugs and kisses handed 'round plentifully as fruit flies in a kitchen in August.

So you can imagine my shock when Mother wrapped her arms tightly around me and hid her face in my hair. "It's irreplaceable, this piano. I didn't know—didn't think I'd ever see it again. But now it's *here*." More sobs, and I dropped my bag to the floor so I could hug her back. "Your father gave it to me, the first Christmas after we were married. I don't know how he managed it!"

That was news to me. I hadn't ever known there was anything particularly special to Mother about this piano. I'd never considered its origins. It had just always been there.

The knowledge felt like a gift.

And also it made me even surer that keeping that ugly note a secret from her was the kindest thing I could do.

APRIL 5, 1927: MONDAY

*T*he second note fell out of my spelling book into my desk at school exactly one week after the first one. When I saw it, it spooked me so much I let my desktop drop, which smashed my finger, which made me yell out one of Mrs. Graham's favorite Inappropriate Words. After a shocked dead silence in the classroom, the teacher sent me to the principal's office for a talking-to.

When I returned, a wave of muffled nervous giggles greeted me. I just held my head high and sat down. The note had been replaced by another in George's handwriting.

> *It's not funny but Mamma will die laughing when she hears why you got sent to the principal.*

I caught George's eye and mouthed DON'T YOU DARE TELL HER. He just grinned.

(George is exceeding proper, I should add. He won't even say things like *darn* or *heck* or *gosh*, let alone the kinds of words Mrs. Graham occasionally uses when she's furious about something and Yiddish would be lost on whoever's listening. I was quite sure George's grin was because he felt I got what was coming to me. Not approval.)

I had to stay in the classroom during recess, writing "Louise Pearson will not use foul language again" one hundred times on the blackboard. I did it three extra times because there was still room. I wondered what Anne Shirley's teacher would have written over Anne if she cursed instead of just smashing that slate over Gilbert's head.

George had made the note disappear, so I didn't get to look more closely at it until we were walking to the Crystal Gardens for our dance lesson.

It was another crude drawing, this time of a scrawny kid with a noose around her neck.

(Me.)

And the words:

DON'T BLAB UGLY SCARECROW.

It gave me gooseflesh all over.

"Sam hanged himself in jail," I whispered, nervously running my thumb along the edge of the paper and giving myself a papercut. "Ow. Who in the world knows these things?"

George looked worried, but he didn't have an answer.

Olivia and Natalia greeted me in the dressing room, but I felt as if I was in a bubble looking out and could only manage a weak smile. As I changed, I caught a glimpse of myself in the mirror and made a face at my reflection.

Don't blab, ugly scarecrow.

I hated the way I looked. The layers of clothes I tried to hide under might have concealed the truth from the general public, but even if nobody else saw what a scrawny, shapeless stick I was, I knew. Dance clothes concealed nothing, so I refused harder than ever to shed my long underwear. They didn't impede my movements, so Mrs. Tabitha didn't complain.

Olivia, on my right, was round and adorable with her head full of curly brown hair that she was tying back with a ribbon, and on my left was the new student Opal with her doll-perfect complexion and striking green eyes. Both girls, without even knowing it, made me feel worse about myself.

I heard Sam's voice in my head. *You're a skinny—* and then a word I won't write down. *You're ugly and nobody will ever want you.* My mother, cowering in a corner, eyes full of tears and terror. It was always her or me, and each wanted to spare the other. It was like Sam had come back from the dead. We'd felt such freedom, such relief, but these notes were bringing it all back to me again.

I backed up to the wall and slid to the floor, hiding my face in my hands, and Olivia and Opal immediately turned to me in concern, crouching to join me and lay gentle hands on my arms. It was sweet of them.

"I'm okay," I said after a minute, even though I was far from okay. I forced myself to my feet, forced a smile at these two girls I hardly knew yet but who were so kind. I loved dance lessons and I was angry that this mysterious note-dropper was trying to ruin this for me.

On the way home, safely ensconced once more in my many layers, I lagged behind George. He turned, walking backwards, to call out, "What are you shauchling for?"

(One of his dad's words. Of course.)

I continued dragging my feet. "You'd be shauchling, too, if you had my misery on your back."

He waited for me to catch up before asking, "How did that note get into your spelling book, anyway?"

"I've been thinking about that. The first time, when I left my bag behind, it could have been anyone, anytime. It was there three days! There are Mrs. Tabitha's other students, plus the regular people who come through on dance evenings, and whoever works there, I guess. But this last time, it had to have been during the lesson, because that's the only time the bag hasn't been with me." I shuddered, wondering if this vile person had a way to watch us girls as we changed. To know when we left the room. I squeezed my eyes shut, refusing to let that one particular memory surface. "I'll check the room next time. See if there's anywhere a person could hide."

"Maybe don't leave your bag where you can't see it, too," George advised.

For a while we walked in silence. "What about other relatives?" George asked. "Sam is dead—are we *sure* he's dead?"

I shuddered again, remembering the call we got not long after Sam had been locked up for bootlegging, when the prison people told Mother they found him hanging in his cell. "Yeah. Your dad went to see the body. Just to reassure us it was true."

"Who else besides him might have a bone to pick with you and your mother?"

I sighed. "All of them? Those Pearsons always hated us. Mother for being an outsider. Daddy for putting her and me first. All three of us for not meekly following along with the herd, I suppose. It could be any of them, but Junction City is ages from here. I never heard of any of them coming to Salem. Whoever it is, it's uncanny how much he seems to know."

Things only Sam and I would know.

"Didn't he have sons?"

"Jim and Hank, yes."

"Could it be one of them?"

"I couldn't be sure. They never lived with us. Jim was arrested when Sam was, but they let him go. Lack of evidence, your dad said. I have no idea what became of him."

"He's a possible suspect, then. And Hank?"

"I don't know. He probably knew about the bootlegging, but he was always around the farm. I don't remember a day where I didn't see him, driving the farm truck around and bossing people, whereas Jim and Sam were gone a lot doing 'business'."

As we were about to turn onto our street, George put a hand on my arm to stop me. "Promise me something," he said.

"What?"

"That you won't go wandering around by yourself. I—don't think it would be safe."

I locked eyes with him. Self-imposed imprisonment was still imprisonment. I knew he was just trying to be protective, and it was sweet, but...

But realistically?

I was bigger than him and if it came down to it, it would be me punching someone where they'd rather not be punched. Not George.

He was doing that puppy eyes thing, though.

I said I was immune, but maybe I lied, because I said:

"Okay."

APRIL 10, 1927: SUNDAY

After a long afternoon of Mother making me refresh my piano skills, George asked me if I wanted to go out with him to listen to a speaker at the Methodist church.

"Are you changing loyalties?" I asked, only half joking, reaching for my hat.

"No," he said, missing the levity completely. "It's a man who calls himself 'the converted Jew'."

We walked through the dim evening streets until we reached the Methodist church and joined the stream of other people entering the building.

Only after we sat down, as near the front as possible, did I realize George had been wearing his kippah under his hat. "What's that for?" I hissed.

"Shameless bid for attention," he whispered back. "If I stand out maybe he'll notice me and I'll have better odds of talking to him."

I should have known we wouldn't be out of here promptly afterwards. Still, it was an escape from Schubert and Bach for a bit, and I honestly didn't much mind.

The speaker's name was Dr. Nathan Cohen Beskin, and even I had to admit he was completely engrossing. He told the story of how he grew up in Russia, about something called pogroms, where the Russian Christians would come into a Jewish community and just slaughter people left and right. It was his only exposure to Christians until much later. *No wonder Jews don't trust Christians,* I thought. And then I wondered if Mrs Graham's Not-Talked-About-Parents had left Russia because of something like that happening in their town. I wished I could ask her, but I didn't think she'd like it if I did.

Dr. Beskin was going to be speaking every evening for the whole week, and promised that the next evening he would talk about how he came to believe in Jesus as Messiah. I wondered if George planned to go every night, then laughed. Of course he wouldn't miss it for the world.

There was a long line of people who wanted to talk with Dr. Beskin afterwards, and I find standing in long lines insufferably boring. Okay, if I had a chance to meet Thea Rasche, I probably wouldn't mind so much. But I didn't need to talk to this man, so I went to the back of the sanctuary where I could still see George but use the pew as a barre to stealthily practice a list of things Mrs. Tabitha had given me particularly to work on.

At last Geroge was the only one still waiting, and Dr. Beskin rubbed his hands together, his thickly accented voice carrying through the room. "Do come sit here with me, young man."

I think they must have talked for at least an hour, heads bent close together over a Bible. The deacon responsible for locking up nodded off in a pew for most of that time. I couldn't hear George's half of the conversation, which was probably all over my head anyway. At last they stood up, and Dr. Beskin insisted that the sleepy, long-suffering deacon drop us home on his way, since it was so late.

"Will you be coming tomorrow night?" Dr. Beskin asked us, as we got out.

"I will," George said, glancing at me, and I shrugged noncommittally. "Every night except Wednesday. I study with Rabbi Zylberman Wednesday nights. Will you come to our seder on Saturday night, sir?"

"It depends what plans the church has made for me," Dr Beskin answered. "I will talk to them and let you know ttomorrow." They shook hands, and we waved as they drove away.

"I think," George said, as we let ourselves in, "that he enjoyed talking to someone who doesn't regard him as a mere curiosity."

"How do you mean?" I asked, following him up the stairs.

"Oh, well... people who look at us Jewish folks like some exotic sideshow attraction, if they bother to notice us at all. Maybe it's like Protestants looking at Catholics, though I don't know any Catholics, so I can't be sure. But something very different, that only interests them as an oddity."

"What did you talk about?"

"Lots. He showed me things about Messiah from the prophets that no Christian had shown me yet. I guess because so many Christians and Jews don't like listening to each other, so they don't know."

"Oh."

He turned dreamily into his room, and I went to look in on Mother.

She was sitting in a rocking chair with one of those portable secretaries on her lap, writing in a composition book. My interest was piqued. Did Mother keep a journal? If so, I'd never known.

She smiled, closing the book. Not in a hurry as if it was something to hide. "How was it?"

"George is over the moon. The speaker was really interesting, though. I might go listen tomorrow too. Anyway, I came to say goodnight."

She smiled again, and I bent down to hug her lightly before turning to go to my own room.

George's drawing of the "Victorian Monstrosity"

April 15, 1927: Friday

On George's advice, I did stop leaving my bag in the dressing room, stowing it instead beside the piano where I could always see it... and the notes stopped coming.

But I was still so anxious all the time, wondering who was carrying on Sam's work for him. The person simply knew too much, and although Sam's sons were the likeliest culprits, I did find it unlikely that either of them would know why "scarecrow" specifically would be the one word to use to get me quaking.

By today I couldn't bear it any more, and I felt so sick, I didn't even ask for permission. I just left school after recess. I didn't tell George. All I wanted was to go curl up in bed and tell Clotilde my troubles.

I walked in the back door. Mrs. Graham had finally finished putting her kitchen back together after a flurry of using up all her *chametz* and *kitniyot* over the past few weeks and completely scrubbing the house clean from top to bottom. (She had explained in great depth to me what both those words meant, but it had seemed extremely complicated, and I'd already forgotten the details. But it was something to do with grains and leaven and certain foods not being eaten during Passover week.) She looked up from the silver she was polishing for tomorrow's seder, and I asked, "Is Mother here?"

"She went to practice on the church organ and fetch me some salmon."

"Alone?" I squeaked out in panic.

"Why not?" Mrs. Graham narrowed her eyes at me. "You don't look well. Are you home early because you're sick? The school hasn't 'phoned."

"I think I ate too many cookies last night," I said. It was the only thing I could think of that wasn't a lie, that might have been a reason for the grinding ache in my middle. We'd had such a surfeit of cookies and pastries that even George conceded defeat and helped me give them away to neighbors.

Mrs. Graham watched me as I left the kitchen, and I went upstairs to the toilet, where I was alarmed to find brown streaks in my underwear, and more on the paper when I wiped. Panicked, I ran back downstairs, hollering.

"Mrs. Graham! I'm dying!"

I wasn't dying, of course. I know about "the curse" from eavesdropping on older girls' whispered conversations. But it's different when it's you, different when you're living in dread for your own and your mother's safety and the last thing you need is for your body to decide to make DRASTIC UNWELCOME CHANGES.

Mrs. Graham's silver clattered to the table at my noise and she nearly collided with me as I ran back into the kitchen. She led me to the little sofa near her bed, sat me down with her, and asked, "What's going on?"

"I'm—I'm bleeding," I whispered. "The curse. I guess that's why I hurt. Not the cookies." *And also I hurt because my life and my mother's life is at risk, and so is yours probably, and George's and Mr. Graham's, and you've sent my mother out alone to buy FISH—*

She gave me a sympathetic look. "First time?" I nodded. "And how much do you know about this?"

"Something to do with... with growing up and having babies?"

She stood up and walked to her worktable, a perpetually untidy heap of miscellany that no one but she ever touched. Out of a stack of books and pamphlets, she extracted a thin little volume and brought it to me.

"Here," she said. "This is decent. This woman has a lot of good things to say. Although I'm not terribly fond of *all* her ideas. She thinks white people are the best and should take over the world, and that inferior ones should be sterilized. You start trying to sterilize people... Negroes, say, or the 'feeble-minded'—who determines if you're feeble-minded, anyway? Then where do you stop? Asians? Jews?

They want us eradicated. But if you just remember that philosophy—it's called eugenics—is a heap of excrement, you can just move on to the better things she has to say. I don't remember there being much of that in this particular book." She saw my alarmed face and softened. "I'm sorry, I'm ranting again, I know. But you ought to understand these things."

I took the book. *What Every Girl Should Know*, by Margaret Sanger. I glanced up as Mrs. Graham sat back down. "You just... have this sitting around?"

She laughed. "I was going to give it to George. Quite frankly, I wanted him to have some scientific accuracy to balance whatever rubbish his father might tell him when I'm not around. But the poor lad got so flustered over the boy one I gave him a few months ago I decided not to torture him with this just yet. He knows it's here when he's ready for it. Anyway, you go on upstairs and have a nice hot bath, and I'll run to the store and fetch you some Kotex, because I haven't used them for some time..."

She untied her apron, swapped her kerchief for a hat, picked up her gloves and handbag and disappeared.

I trudged upstairs and ran the bath. It did feel lovely to sit in hot water. I opened the book, careful to keep it dry, and began to read. I skipped over the introduction, because it had a lot of words I couldn't figure out, but after that it was fairly simple to read. This was a relief, as I'd sooner have died than ask George to read it to me, and I wasn't sure if I knew Olivia well enough yet to ask her, to admit that on top of being unattractive I was also stupid. (Did my reading troubles count as "feeble-mindedness", I wondered? And what was *sterilization*, anyway?)

I also wondered what "boy book" George had been given. He might not want to read it, but *I* was certainly curious. I'd have to poke around some Wednesday night when he was with Rabbi Zylberman.

I was so absorbed in my book and my thoughts that the knock on the bathroom door started me. It opened a crack, and Mrs. Graham's hand reached in to set the parcel on the floor, just inside the door. "I've left some aspirin and water for you in your room, in case it gets to hurting a lot."

"Thanks," I said shyly.

And since that bath was going cold anyway, I got out, dried off, opened the Kotex, and wrangled a while with the pins and straps on the accompanying belt until it was positioned how it ought to be. I wondered how long I was supposed to go before changing it. I'd have to ask, if I couldn't figure it out myself. Maybe the book would tell me. Or I could ask my mother.

Where *was* Mother? It oughtn't take this long to buy salmon.

Unless she'd forgotten it, playing. (Entirely possible.)

I climbed under my covers, pulled them up to my chin, and curled around Clotilde, deep in thought. The cramps weren't unbearable, but they certainly weren't *fun*. "I don't want to grow up," I whispered to Clotilde. "Not if it means unpleasantness like this. I just want the old-enough-for-flying-lessons part." Another thought came to me then. "Except I do want babies someday, so I guess that means I have to put up with this. I wonder how long it goes on. It must stop eventually, since Mrs. G says she doesn't need Kotex anymore. She's forty-nine. Mother's thirty-five. I don't know about her. I guess that means at least twenty-three years of this. It seems an awfully long time. If you had one baby every year... nobody needs twenty-three babies! Not even me. It seems silly you can't just turn it on and off..."

I must have dozed, because the next thing I knew was being jolted awake by a knocking at my door.

"Louise!" George's voice. "Are you decent? Are you alive? I've been banging for ages!"

Disoriented, I sat up, just enough presence of mind left to quickly stuff the Kotex box under my pillow.

"I'm alive," I said sleepily.

"I thought you were kidnapped!" he said, sweeping in dramatically. "I was all ready to walk home and suddenly realized you weren't with me—"

Two seconds of dead silence.

"You didn't notice I was gone until you were ready to walk home?" I asked.

"Well... no," he admitted. "It took all my brains to get through arithmetic. Are you sick?"

"I don't feel well," I said primly, annoyed at his oblivion to my absence. "What if I *had* been kidnapped and you didn't notice 'til you were ready to come home? 'Oh Louise!! Don't go wandering town alone, it's not safe!' The gangster would've had a three hours' start on you, at least!"

He dropped his gaze to the floor. "Sorry," he said. "I'll try to pay more attention."

"Fine watchdog you make," I muttered.

"All the more reason Mamma ought to let me get an actual watchdog," he said, brightening.

His cheer infuriated me. "Oh, just go away," I snapped, and burrowed back down until I was completely engulfed by quilt. I stayed there until I heard the soft click of the door latch as he left.

At dinnertime, Mother came up to see me. I still felt blah, but I was relieved she was home safely.

"Oh, you're awake!" she said. "I came up earlier and you weren't. Alice told me. I'm so glad she was here to help you—I wish I'd known—do you feel better? Shall I bring you some supper up? A hot water bottle?"

"I don't feel like eating just yet," I said. "I'll come down for something later. But the hot water bottle sounds nice."

"All right," Mother said. I hoped she'd cross the room to sit with me, that we would have a moment of open communication where she initiated me into all the secrets of womanhood. But she just hesitated in the doorway, twisting her wedding ring like she does sometimes when she's anxious. So I broke the silence.

"You didn't say anything to George?"

Her shock was palpable. "Of course not! What business is it of his? Anyway, he's not even here. He went to hear that Jewish man speaking again."

I knew she wouldn't have, and I smiled. "Thanks," I said, nestling back into my pillow, to wait for her return with the promised bottle.

Around nine o'clock I sneaked downstairs to find something to eat. Mr. and Mrs. Graham still had one lamp on, the one by their bed. Its light was just enough for me to navigate the kitchen.

I'd been planning to make a sandwich, but as soon as I opened the breadbox I remembered all the bread in the house would be the flat kind for a week. Heaving a sigh, I got myself a plate and piled it with two smallish carrots, a chunk of cheese, a couple inches of elk sausage, and some of the matzah cracker things from the cupboard, then made my silent way upstairs to my room, where I put on Daddy's sweater and settled cross-legged on my bed. I snapped open my pocket knife, neatly slicing the cheese and sausage to make haphazard cracker sandwiches.

I always found the mental image of Mr. Graham hunting elk, or anything really, the height of hilarity for some reason. He was always so posh and polished-looking, and I could not for the life of me picture him crawling through underbrush in hunting regalia. I giggled aloud as I popped my first bite into my mouth and wondered if he'd consider taking me along when he went this fall. I didn't know how to fire a gun, but surely that could be remedied.

Downstairs the front door opened and closed, and a few minutes later I heard George coming upstairs. My door was ajar and he stuck his head in. "You okay, Lou?" he asked softly. "You've been acting kind of weird."

"I'm fine." I was still annoyed at his obliviousness, but there was no point in discussing it now.

He paused. "I'm sorry I didn't notice you were gone. Truly. I'm sick thinking how bad it could have been, and it would have been my fault."

I kept eating my sandwiches in silence, letting him marinate in his regret.

"Could I read you something?" he asked, his forlorn face melting my resistance in spite of myself.

"Okay," I said, making sure to sound as if I was only humoring him, but his face lit up.

"Anything you want!"

I stifled a snigger at the idea of handing him *What Every Girl Should Know*, but I'd had enough of that already today to last me a while. So I thought over the options on his shelves. I really wanted to hear the mystery stories, but just now, more than anything, I wanted a comforting escape.

Something I already knew the ending of would be safest.

"Zenda," I said.

He'd read it to me twice since we'd been friends, and I knew it was one of his favorites too, so he wouldn't be bothered by my wanting to revisit it. Princess Flavia was my heroine, because she didn't throw duty and honor to the wind, even for true love. It takes great strength of character to be so steadfast, especially with Rudolf Rassendyll being such a dream.

(George read me the sequel, too, but I prefer to pretend it doesn't exist and I never heard of it. Only happy endings for my Flavia! Where

she and Rudolf find a way to retain their honor and dignity but also kiss a lot and have a bunch of adorable redheaded babies.)

(George says that's unrealistic, ridiculous, and disgustingly soppy. I DON'T CARE.)

He went to fetch the book and his pillow and a blanket, which he wrapped around his shoulders like a cape. I settled in under my own covers with my plate on my lap, to slowly finish my supper. I saved the carrots for last, reasoning that they could act as my toothbrush and save me getting out of bed again.

"'I wonder when in the world you're going to do anything, Rudolf?'" George began.

He was so good with voices. He could turn on and off his parents' accents like there was a switch, and it delighted me to no end. I tried very hard to stay awake after the last carrot, but before Rudolf had spent his "four and twenty hours in Paris", I had fallen asleep.

April 16, 1927: Saturday

*I*n the morning I felt quite myself again. The bleeding had stopped. Was that all there was to this, then? If so, it wasn't so bad. I could put up with this for twenty-odd years.

Still, I wore my brown dress, just in case it started again and anything leaked.

And I combed my hair more carefully than usual. If I was growing up, I decided, it was time to care more about my hair.

The reflection of my colorless pale locks drooping limply on either side of my colorless pale face wasn't very promising. I wished I had Princess Flavia's glorious red tresses instead.

My hair had never taken curl, and Mother had given up trying years ago. Running my fingers through it this morning, though, I thought its texture seemed less soft and flyaway than it used to. Perhaps it would be worth trying again.

It was an interesting day. Mrs. Graham was busy in the kitchen preparing to host the seder, to which Rabbi Zylberman and his family and the three Wisniewskis and Dr. Beskin would all be coming. Mrs. Graham wasn't entirely thrilled about Dr. Beskin's inclusion, but she told George it would be on his own head if the man stirred up any trouble or offended the rabbi. George expressed positivity that the reverend doctor would do neither of these things, although his eyes seemed to indicate a tiny bit of uncertainty, and my own impression of the man was that he was not exactly the head of the Tact and Diplomacy Department. But Mrs. Graham's next comment reminded me that neither is she, particularly.

"Well, you remind him when you let him in that his Jesus can just wait on the doorstep until we're through here!"

"Jesus won't mind," George replied easily. "He can chat with Elijah while he waits."

Mrs. Graham shot him a Look.

George knew he was treading a fine line, and I knew it hurt him a little. He wanted to please everyone, that was his problem.

He and I were put to work adding extra leaves to the dining table, spreading out her white lace tablecloth, and setting fourteen places using the silver, china, and crystal that had all been washed and polished yesterday: beautiful things that Mrs. Graham had brought all the way from England and hung on to through all their years of grinding poverty.

(The fourteenth place was for Elijah, said George.

"So we're setting a place for someone who won't actually be sitting there?"

"Well, it would never do for him to walk in and not find the place waiting for him, would it?"

I decided not to push it.)

Mrs. Graham was funny. Technically she shouldn't have been doing all this (and the cooking) because it was the Sabbath, but as strictly as she followed some rules (the ones involving food, mostly), there were others she completely (or selectively) disregarded.

"I pick my battles," she'd said when I asked her about it. "I'm too tired to be MY PARENTS and do everything." She said "my parents" as if it was a curse. "I may never not be too tired again."

"Maybe if you actually took Shabbat off, you'd be less tired," George said. It was their bone of contention to pick together at every possible opportunity, but this day she snapped that on this particular Sabbath, she was proclaiming the fifth commandment as more important and You Can Just Fold These Napkins and Hush Already, Georgie.

(He *hates* when she calls him Georgie.)

"And you can just decline to mention tonight that we did all this today," she said sternly at both of us. "It's bad enough that you're bringing in that apostate, and I am not in the mood to have an argument with the rabbi this evening."

I smothered a laugh. It was impossible for them to be in the same room and not argue.

I went out to the garden to gather up the best of the tulips and daffodils and a few of the bloomiest forsythia twigs to decorate the table while George made place cards.

Despite all Mrs. Graham's fuss, everything was ready in plenty of time, and there was no conflict. George took Dr. Beskin aside when he let him in and they had a brief whispered conversation, which must have done the trick, because he didn't mention Jesus once all evening.

Mrs. Graham had made seared salmon with lemon and a delicious dill dressing, and the matzah and charoset and other things. The Zylbermans came bearing a heaping platter of mandelbrot and lots of grape juice. Mrs. Tabitha had a giant, freshly-baked potato kugel in hand. Clearly Mrs. Graham wasn't the only one who didn't mind cooking on the Sabbath.

This was the first proper seder I'd been to. Last year, Mrs. Graham had done a simplified version to ease herself back into it. She'd always quietly done her deleavening, but there her energy had always given out, and she really was trying to do her part to teach her son at home and not leave it all to Rabbi Zylberman.

When she had first introduced us to the Friday night Sabbath rituals, Mrs. Graham had explained everything as she went along, translating the Hebrew prayers to English for us. Now George did the translating himself, but also there were enough of the little grey Haggadahs so we could all stay on track with what was going on. This was good for those of us, such as Mr. Graham, who didn't speak or read any Hebrew.

I'd learned this story in Sunday school, of course—how the Israelites were slaves in Egypt and God sent plague after plague when Pharaoh refused to set them free, and how the final plague was death to every firstborn child, unless the family had obeyed God by putting lamb's blood on the doorframe. The destroying angel would pass over those houses. I always thought how scary that sounded, being a firstborn myself, but aside from that it was just another Bible story.

But taking part in this thing with Jewish people made me see the story differently. It was the words "Next year at this season may the whole house of Israel be free!" that got to me. This story was about *their ancestors*, not just some abstract group of slaves to which I, for instance, had no connection. They might not still be slaves, but they are still hated and mistrusted and discriminated against by so many. It all just hit me very suddenly why Mrs. Graham is so outspoken about the perception of Jews by non-Jews. She wants me and Mother to understand and be allies, instead of enemies, like Sam and his ilk.

When it was all over and everyone had gone home, I lay in bed a while thinking about things, wondering which faith George would settle with in the end, and whether I would want to be that with him.

George's parents were making it work, not being the same. But George was different. I felt sure that for him it would be all or nothing, and he would eventually grow up and marry someone and he would want that someone to believe the same way he did, so the children didn't feel so torn apart, like he did.

It was a little scary, thinking that way. Wondering how far I'd be willing to go to keep the precious friendship we had.

And... possibly... someday be the person he wanted to marry.

Mrs Louise Graham has rather a nice ring to it, I think.

MAY 13, 1927: FRIDAY

*T*wo French aviators who tried to cross the Atlantic from Paris to New York last weekend didn't make it. They are lost, and I feel just sick about it. The paper claims there is still hope, but I know they are dead—and of course George made sure I didn't miss the news.

In spite of that disaster, and some others recently, several Americans are in New York City right now, intending to make their own attempts to win the $25,000 that a man named Raymond Orteig is offering to the first person to cross from New York to Paris (or Paris to New York).

Here are the men who have tried and failed:
1. Noel Davis and Stanton Hall Wooster, dead in a test crash April 27, 1927. They were US Navy airmen, and their plane was a K-47 Keystone Pathfinder named "American Legion".
2. Charles Nungesser and François Coli, from France, in a Levasseur PL.8 biplane called "The White Bird". (Mr. Graham says the original French would be *L'oiseau blanc,* which makes English seem less crazy, because guess what? It's *not* pronounced LOUISE OOH BLANK. If this and ballet have taught me anything, it is that French is RIDICULOUS.)

Here are the men who are still planning to try:
1. Richard Byrd, Floyd Bennet, and George Noville in a Fokker plane named "America".
2. Clarence Chamberlin and Lloyd Bertaud in a Bellanca

monoplane named "Columbia".
3. Charles Lindbergh in a Ryan single-seater monoplane,
   no name given.

Nobody seems to really know who Charles Lindbergh is. He kind of just... appeared in the papers, without any of the hullabaloo they've made over Byrd's and Chamberlin's teams. Maybe they don't bother because it's unlikely a single flyer will make it on his own.

I wonder how Mr. Orteig feels, knowing that four men have already died for a chance at that money he offered.

I wonder if the other six men will also die grasping for that prize.

It is all rather morbid to think about. Even I admit that. I know flying isn't without risks.

I'm writing all this at my desk in class because I already finished my arithmetic test and I want to look busy. Also I'm very nervous right now and somehow this is forcing me to be rational, writing about aerial destruction/the potential thereof.

Remember how I started not leaving my bags in the dressing room? It stopped the notes coming there. But today—okay, let me start by saying it is both Friday the 13th and also Straw Hat Day, the day we get to put away our winter things and wear summery clothes instead. Mr. Graham brought George and me fresh straw hats last night (mine is really lovely, with a black band and blue silk flowers on) and said he'd be looking for us at the parade today.

Opal and Olivia went with us to watch, but it ended up being impossible to find Mr. Graham in the "straw-hatted madding crowd" (George's words), but we did try to get close to his office. It was gloriously noisy and I cheered myself hoarse. Even George actually paid attention. He never let go of my arm, either, knowing how easily the crowd could pull us apart.

When the parade passed, we had to hurry to get back to school, but the crowd seemed immovable, and in all the jostling, Olivia and Opal got separated from us. I took my hat off and fanned myself with it, and something blue fluttered to my feet. I thought it might be one of the silk flowers, but when I looked, it was a blue piece of card folded in half. I froze, but George stooped to pick it up and unfolded it when I refused to touch it. I read the message over his shoulder.

YOUR UNLUCKY DAY

I'm so scared. Whoever the person is was close enough to tuck that thing into my hat, and I never noticed, and that's just *awful* to think about.

Maybe I should tell Mr. Graham.

Now, I like Mr. Graham, I really do. He's kind and funny, but somehow it's hard to broach serious subjects with him. George manages, but it's his father, which I think makes it easier for him. I don't even know how I'd begin explaining. I could ask George to talk to him for me—and he would—but how much could even Mr. Graham do, really? It might just end up with all the adults being worried and not letting us go anywhere anymore.

It's not fair, George having his paper route and being free and nobody bothering him. I wonder if other girls feel trapped like this, too, or if it's just another way I'm weird and messed up. I had thought the ballet lessons would make me feel freer (and in a way they do), but it still doesn't mean I can go do things ALONE, like George can. Alone-out-of-the-house.

Mrs. Tabitha has begun leaving Natalia with me on the afternoons I don't have lessons, since Natalia's lessons are the same times as mine and she gets bored sitting through lessons that aren't hers. (She's just beginning, like George and Margie and Opal and me, which is why we're all together, and Olivia is there to give us something to strive towards. There's another class of more advanced students that has begun coming down from Portland on Wednesdays for a three-hour lesson because the chance to study with someone like Mrs. Tabitha is a big deal.) When school is out and she adds in some morning classes, Mrs. T says I can keep Natalia then, too. She's taking the cost out of my lessons, which doesn't help my airplane fund, but Natalia is a darling, and it's led to two other mothers asking me to look after theirs, and I do get to keep that money. It may not bring me independence, but it is nice to feel trusted.

Also, it's almost laughable how terrified of small humans George is. He vaporizes within minutes of their arrival and only emerges again after they've all gone. Mr. Graham, on the other hand, seems to adore the children as much as I do. When he's home, he often lingers in the sitting room with me, as much interested in their shenanigans as the children themselves. Mrs. Graham stepped in to ask, very dryly, how much she owed me for minding her husband, and we all had a good laugh over that.

May 21, 1927: Saturday

*T*wo rival topics of interest at the Pearson-Graham breakfast table this morning:

1. LINDBERGH NOW PASSING OVER OCEAN WASTES
2. FOR SALE—FOX TERRIER PUPPIES

Lindbergh Now Passing Over Ocean Wastes

He is DOING IT. He is actually FLYING TO FRANCE. Charles Lindbergh, the person nobody ever heard of until a couple weeks ago, the only man who's crazy enough to try it alone. I am in jitters just imagining it. All that water. It took us DAYS to cross all that water in a ship last year. Just think, if he makes it, what that means for the future of travel!

There were a million items in this morning's paper about Mr. Lindbergh, but I had to struggle through them on my own as best I could, because SOMEBODY who could have READ THEM TO ME was too busy campaigning for

For Sale—Fox Terrier Puppies

The Somebody in question, flushed with excitement, turned the Bright Hopeful Eyes to his father and begged like a baby in a candy shop.

"PLEASE DAD, DAD YOU PROMISED. DAAAADDDD."

(He really has not gotten over Mrs. Graham's callous disposal of his old dog Peach, the minute we were off to Scotland last year.)

Mr. Graham took the page George was shoving in his direction and examined the listing. "Fox terrier puppies, both sexes, nicely marked, pure bred, priced cheap to move quickly." He looked up with amusement. "Any idea how energetic a fox terrier is, son?"

"I don't care, I want one!"

I sat back and watched as both Georges turned matching puppylike eyes to Mrs. Graham, who narrowed her own.

"I do not want a dog," she said flatly, and left the dining room without another word, to where Mother was preparing a batch of wallpaper paste in the kitchen. She was going to hang paper in the unused bedroom upstairs—pinky rosy paper, UGH.)

"She didn't say no," Mr. Graham mused softly in George's direction. "She just said she didn't want a dog."

"I heard that!" Mrs. Graham's voice came from the kitchen.

Mr. Graham winked at George. "Well, it's Saturday and I don't have to work. I don't suppose Louise wants to come along to Not Get a Dog?"

Louise did want to come along, thank you very much.

After Mr. Graham had telephoned to make sure the dog-selling lady would be at home, we all piled into the car, me with newspaper still in hand, which I shoved at George to read me everything about Mr. Lindbergh—who, it seems, is even more boring than George in real life. Apart from the flying planes part.

I guess we just need more GIRLS in planes to liven things up.

Anyway, it took about three-quarters of an hour to get to the address in Jefferson, south of Salem. We pulled into the driveway and Mr. Graham got out and knocked briskly at the front door. When a woman answered, he smoothly doffed his hat and poured on the charm for her. "Mrs. Frank Jones, I presume? We are responding to your advertisement about the fox terrier pups."

He stresses a different syllable than Americans do—ad*ver*tisement—and Mrs. Frank Jones succumbed to the Scottish charm of this debonair stranger like every other woman in the world. "You're the one who rang earlier," she said, patting her hair into place and throwing her apron somewhere off to the side, out of sight. "I recognize your voice." She led us to an outbuilding, chattering all the while about the pups' parentage, while Mr. Graham asked intelligent questions, and George and I trailed along behind, amused.

We dropped to our knees beside the romping puppies. "They're eight weeks old and need to go as fast as possible," Mrs. Jones said. "Didn't intend to have a batch right now, and Mr. Jones was right put out about it. So busy this time of year and all. The last thing we need is these! But the dog escaped from his pen and what with one thing and another—" She gestured helplessly with her hands.

"Which are the boys?" George asked. "It wouldn't do to take home a bitch who'll have puppies and make Mamma really mad—what? It's not cursing if you're talking dogs!"

His father had burst into laughter. "No, it's not, but I still never expected to hear it from you." He joined us on the floor, helping make grabs for puppies until they'd found the two boys. George sat cross-legged with both on his lap, letting them crawl over him while I cuddled the rejected… *girls*…, privately impressed that George had the sense to think ahead that much.

Until I remembered that he was very familiar with the multiplication properties of free-roaming livestock, having had a cow as well as being quite the chicken fancier while still living in Turner. He was just being practical.

"This one," George said at last, after watching the two male puppies for a solid ten minutes as they romped and played around

him and on him. The one he chose kept coming back to him, wagging his stumpy tail and putting on a look of forlorn hope uncannily like George's own expression at the breakfast table earlier that morning. "Take me home with you," he seemed to be begging.

Mr. Graham picked him up, inspected him thoroughly, and at last nodded his approval. "A very fine specimen indeed," he agreed. He quietly handed over the money—a lot of money for a dog that was "priced cheap", I thought—and I wondered if Mrs. Graham would be Having Words with him about it later.

"What will you name him?" I asked, as we climbed into the back seat with the puppy.

George was dreadful about naming things. More often than not, he named his animals after food, except for Moo the cow. "Please don't name it Woof," I said. "Or anything to do with food. Actually I think you should let me name it."

"Depends what you come up with," he said.

I huffed at the stupidity of that remark. As if anything HE came up with would be interesting! I said, "We will name him after whichever aviator makes it across the Atlantic first. Lindbergh, probably, unless he cracks up, then maybe it'll be Chamberlin or Byrd—"

"No dog of mine will be named Byrd," George scoffed. "That's like naming a cat Fysh."

"Says the one who named his favorite chicken Triscuit," I retorted.

He shrugged. "Triscuits are tasty. And Buff Orpingtons are sort of Triscuit-colored."

"I don't even want to think about what awful names your children will end up with someday. 'What did I have for breakfast today? Oh yes, Wheatena, what a perfect name for my brand-new daughter! Hello, everyone, meet Wheatena Graham, a perfect friend for her older brother, Crackers Graham—'"

"Shut up," he said, but he was blushing and laughing. He knew I was right. "Anyway, I already used Wheatena once. For a chicken."

The puppy climbed to the floor of the back seat and sniffed around. His coat was mostly white, with ears and tail and a saddle-shaped spot on his back all the color of perfectly toasted toast. Then he was back on George's lap, leaping to lick his face, then to me to lick

94

mine. I am not generally a huge fan of being slurped on by dogs, but this one was pretty cute.

"We can make a rope and pulley system to bring him up to your room in a basket tonight," I said. "Like the clothesline I made you out your window at The Dump. Then your mother needn't get her knickers in a wad."

Mr. Graham snort-laughed at that from the front. "Well, let's stop on the way home for your pulleys and a basket, then. And a lead and collar."

The man in the store asked what name should go on the tag for the collar, but George shook his head and offered only the bewildering response, "Nobody's made it to Paris yet. Next week."

Mrs. Graham was not impressed when we returned, instructing us to "get that animal a doghouse immediately, because he's not coming in on my clean floors".

So Mr. Graham went shopping again. George and the puppy played happily in the garden while I stealthily executed Operation Pulley Rope from his bedroom window.

Mother was happily humming to herself in the unused bedroom with her wallpaper project. (She is very good at hanging wallpaper.) It was the first time I'd seen her so cheerful in ages, and the room looked much nicer, even if the wallpaper was pink.

"I'll move in here when it's done so I can paper the room I'm sleeping in," she told me when I stepped in to watch.

"This paper isn't going in my room, is it?"

"No," she said, beaming at me, her hair sliding out of the confines of her wallpaper-pasty kerchief. "Yours is having blue and gold stripes."

"Oh, good," I said, smiling back. "Don't fall off the ladder!"

On returning home with the doghouse, Mr. Graham went indoors to let Mrs. Graham Have Words with him (there were many, *many* words) and when she was through, he passed the rest of the afternoon pleasantly in the garden with us, enjoying the puppy almost more than George was, and helping us teach him the chickens were off-limits.

"Don't worry, doggie," I whispered to him when he flopped onto my legs for a brief nap. "You get to sleep in George's room. This one down here is just your *pretend* house."

George and his father grinned conspiratorially.

MAY 22, 1927: SUNDAY

*T*he next morning, George came pounding up the stairs and on my door and didn't even wait for an answer before bursting in, waving the newspaper and dropping to my bed beside me. "He won!"

I stared at him sleepily from under my eyelashes. "Who won what?"

"Charles Lindbergh! He got to Paris!"

That woke me up. I snatched the paper, and all the type began to swim around, but eventually my eyes found Mr. Lindbergh's name, and I used my hands to block out the columns on either side so I could concentrate on what mattered.

> LINDBERGH WELCOMED IN FRANCE—25,000 Enthusiastic People Greet Lone Aviator at Le Bourget Field—CITIES STAGING CELEBRATIONS—Average Speed 113 Miles an Hour for 3000 Miles—RECORDS BROKEN—Spontaneous Celebrations Are Held on Receipt of News; Congratulations Sent by President Coolidge and Others

I squeaked happily, bouncing. "Read the rest to me," I begged, pushing the paper back his way, leaning in close, following his finger along the text as he read.

Mr. Lindbergh arrived in Paris at 10:21 PM after 33 ½ hours in the air. There were so many people at the airfield waiting to greet him, he got actually CARRIED away from his plane! The poor man just wanted sleep, I bet, not thousands of people up in his business. (I don't think I could stay awake that long if I tried.) Anyway, he made it! Alive! And that is what counts.

"I guess the dog has a name now," George said, folding up the paper. "It's getting late, though. Better hurry if you want breakfast before church. I need to go make sure *Lindbergh* isn't trying to eat the chickens."

I had trouble thinking of anything but Mr. Lindbergh, all through breakfast and church too, as I stared up at the ceiling and imagined being suspended between sky and sea, powered forward by the magical machine called an airplane.

MAY 25, 1927: WEDNESDAY

George is at Rabbi Z's and I'm all by myself in my room, bored, but not wanting Mother to know that because she'll tell me to go practice more SCHUBERT. So I'm going to write in my journal.

Between the new puppy and the news of Charles Lindbergh's success, I'd completely forgotten about the Straw Hat Day note until I was gathering up laundry for Mother this morning and found it in the pocket of the dress I wore that day.

Despite the threat, nothing actually unlucky had befallen me that day, but I still shivered. I also noticed the paper had a smell, vaguely floral, as if my stalker had pulled the card out of some grandmother's stationery drawer. I fished the other two notes out of Clotilde and sniffed them. Same scent. It wasn't lavender or rose. I couldn't place it. Mrs. Graham would know, but I'd have to show her, and that would never do. She's twice proved an ally to me since being here, but I'm not sure how far I can trust that to go.

I decided to forget about it until later and buried all three back inside Clotilde, but it's been nagging at me anyway, ever since.

Let's think of something cheerful now! This morning there was a fun new headline:

HONORS HEAPED ON YANKEE FLIER; KISS BESTOWED

I think that's the best headline I've ever read. The story was that Mr. Lindbergh got kissed by some French woman and it made him blush. George rolled his eyes as he read it to me—read it rather faster than is his custom, I might add.

I've been thinking a lot about kisses. Opal asked me in whispers at our last lesson, as we were changing back into our street clothes afterwards, if George had ever kissed me.

I am afraid I howled with laughter at the idea.

George had no interest in "spit swapping" last summer, I know. Because I became besotted with his cousin Vincent, and George said he couldn't imagine what on earth could be appealing about getting that close to a girl, let alone slopping their mouths all over each other's faces. "Dis-*gusting*," he said. "And anyway, Vincent's almost grown up, don't be an idiot."

Prior to meeting Vincent, I'd have agreed with George about the appeal of kisses, but something about Vincent just... bowled me over. (I think he has that effect on most girls, and it's probably what got him into the mysterious trouble that everybody avoided talking about when we were there, but whatever it was got him expelled from the school he'd been attending.)

I asked Vincent to kiss me, but he refused, with hearty and offensive laughter. "Father would tan me and turn me into a hearthrug if I even *contemplated* kissing an eleven year old kid. And anyway I wouldn't, any more than I'd bother any of those other lassies Father's taken in."

He was seventeen. Like George said, practically grown up. It would have been weird, but at the time I didn't see it that way, because I'd lost my head. Now, of course, I'd like to sink into the floor remembering my audacious and utterly inappropriate request.

So I told Opal that no, George hadn't, and wasn't likely to. Olivia, who had been listening in rapt attention, looked relieved.

She's gone sweet on George the past couple weeks. Ever since the seder, I think. I don't think he's even noticed, which would drive me bonkers if I was Olivia. Heck, it drives me bonkers as *me*. She's always gazing dreamily at him. I can't exactly blame her, as he is rather pleasing to the eyes, but George is mine, and when it comes to this sort of thing, I find myself incredibly unwilling to share him.

But, based on his reaction to that item about Mr. Lindbergh getting kissed, it appears that George's opinions on "spit swapping" are unchanged, so perhaps I'm worrying needlessly about Olivia As Potential Threat.

(Interesting that George doesn't seem to mind slobbery dog kisses, though.)

I keep thinking back to that day I found the first note, and how sweetly devoted and kind George was to me, and the little flutters I got watching his placid profile against the light in my window, and I want desperately to find out what is so exciting and special about kissing.

But I want to find out with George, nobody else.

And I don't want Olivia to get to him first.

But also... also I have a secret that I am ashamed of and I don't know if George would ever want me if he knew.

I've gone from feeling incredibly happy to feeling as if I'm drowning in despair in just a matter of seconds.

I think I'll write about that secret. It might matter, if the person writing the notes manages to nab me like I suspect he plans to, because Uncle Jamie won't hear in time to speak for me, and he's the only person I've told.

When I was ten—the summer I met George, the day his Uncle Jamie tried and failed to take on Sam and rescue me—that was when the Really Horrible Thing happened, or at least it *could* have been Really Horrible. Afterwards I started to question whether it might have been worse and maybe I was overreacting, but Uncle Jamie just said, "Of course it could have been worse, but that doesn't make what *did* happen less evil."

I already wrote how my father died. What I didn't know at the time, but afterwards learned, was that Daddy had discovered the secret of Sam's bootlegging operation. It had been carefully kept from Daddy, because Sam must have known he would never have stood for it, that he'd report it if he found out. That's why Sam killed him—to silence him. He killed him because the riches he was obtaining illegally were more important to him than his own cousin's life.

Marrying my mother was related, too. Sam had a plan. Mr.

Graham explained to me that, as his wife, Mother wouldn't be compelled to testify against him in court, and Sam was confident he could keep her (and me) intimidated enough that we wouldn't *want* to, if it ever came to that.

But Sam hadn't counted on an upstart earl from Scotland (Uncle Jamie) and the upstart earl's brother (Mr. Graham) interfering. Men who weren't about to be intimidated. Sam's empire of illicit booze-peddling was crumbling down around him, and his fury and fear drove him to drinking his own poison, and being drunk made him more violent, and more careless in the way he showed that violence.

This is the reason I find the notes so scary, and why I feel my stomach drop to the floor and my heart leap to my throat each time a new one shows up: Sam's casual violence. The way he *simply didn't care* how his actions affected anyone but himself. The notes bother George, but they *terrify* me.

It's as if Sam hanging himself in prison never really happened. As if somehow he's still out there roaming free, waiting for his chance to destroy Mother and me from off the face of the earth.

Darn it, I don't want to write this.

Okay, I practiced ballet for a bit to calm myself down and found a piece of cord to put that crackerjack fish charm onto as a necklace so I can fiddle with it with my free hand while I write. It's not quite like having George here, but he did give it to me, so maybe it can remind me to be brave. And I'm getting tired. Maybe the words will come more easily now.

The Really Horrible Thing happened the Sunday when Uncle Jamie challenged Sam—at church, right after services, in plain view of the exiting worshippers. He only said one word to Sam—"No"—when Sam grabbed my shoulder to force me to come with him. Uncle Jamie took Sam's arm to restrain him, but Sam managed to shake him off, scooped me up like a sack of potatoes, threw me into the back of the car, tearing off home before I could even sit up, and before Uncle Jamie had time to get to me again.

And as soon as we got home, despite the warmth of the day, Sam shut all the windows to ensure that no neighbors would hear. Then he undid his belt, laid me over the piano bench, and lashed me twenty times, across my legs and on up. It took him a long time to get to twenty, because I am good at dodging, and I was getting too big for him to hold me down and still successfully hit me with the belt. He was furious that I wouldn't just lie down and take it.

I am not like my mother.

Perhaps that was when he realized that he would have to move on to worse things.

Anyway, when he finally got to twenty, the three of us had burnt soup, and I could swear Mother was trying to be invisible in case he

decided to lash out at her about the soup.

I couldn't sit, so I ate mine kneeling on a stool, glaring, wishing I dared throw the contents of my bowl in his face.

Then he told Mother and me to sit in the living room (or, in my case, drape myself stomach down over the sofa's armrest) and we spent the entire hot, stuffy, miserable rest of the day there under his watchful eye as he swilled stuff from a jug and got drunker and drunker.

Mother's fingertips almost imperceptibly played some tune on her knees. It was something she often did when she was anxious, and her eyes stayed closed—either because she was praying or because she couldn't stand the sight of Sam. Possibly both.

As twilight fell, Sam got up to switch on the lights, never taking his eyes off us as he did it. The welts on my legs burned and itched, and I longed to escape upstairs to my room, but I didn't want to risk it.

Turner's power plant shut down at eight o'clock every night, so the clock chimed eight times into the sudden darkness that engulfed us. Here it was, I thought. My chance to escape. Sam hadn't thought to light the oil lamps in advance. He wouldn't see.

But he was, surprisingly, still quick enough on his feet to block the doorway in advance of my reaching it, and he gripped my upper arm so tightly, I winced.

"Light the lamps, Lydia." Sam's voice was calm and quiet. An unsettling thing, considering how he usually got so loud and aggressive when he was drunk.

I heard Mother feeling her way toward the nearest lamp. A match hissed into flame, and then a second one, and then a third. It was too much; one lamp was sufficient to see by. But he wanted it as bright as possible.

"Hey," he said to me, his expression leering. I saw him catch my mother's eye, from where she had sunk into a corner armchair, looking ghostly in the lamplight, her elbows resting on her knees and her hands over her mouth, as if she was afraid she might scream and would need to hold it back. Once Sam was sure he had her attention, he slowly and deliberately lifted my skirt from the back and put his hand down my pants. He kept it there, motionless, holding Mother's horrified gaze like a snake with its prey, and said:

"I saw you today, Lydia. I saw you looking at him. You thought he dropped from heaven to save you, didn't you? Like some *angel*." His eyes got squinty-dark, and he went on. "You ever cross me, Lydia— you ever even *try* to speak to that [nasty word] earl across the way—it won't be my hand down here."

I didn't understand what Sam meant. Not then. But the feeling of his hand against my bare behind made my skin crawl, felt so dirty and wrong that I didn't have to understand. I'd have screamed then, if fear for my mother's safety hadn't kept me silent. I was not going to let him hurt her, no matter what he did to me. He mustn't hurt Mother. Hadn't she already suffered enough, losing Daddy so horribly?

Hadn't I?

I shuddered when Sam turned his eyes back to mine, the same pale Pearson blue as my own. "And you? If you want to protect your mother, you'll do what I say. You have to pay for what you want, you hear me? Pay for her safety. Nothing's free, you scrawny little [nastier word]. No one will ever want you anyway, *scarecrow*."

He stumbled a little then, loosening his hold on my arm just enough in steadying himself that I was able to pull free of his other hand, dart under his arm and up to my room, barricading the door with my bureau to slow his entrance if he tried to come in. To alert me in time to escape out the window. (He'd ripped out the doorknob a few weeks prior, to prevent me from locking him out, as I'd done in the past.)

My heart was racing, and my hands shook so much as I changed into my nightgown that I gave up on the buttons and tried to find a comfortable position under my covers. And then I lay wide awake in the dark, long after the sound of Mother's prolonged weeping in the next room had been eclipsed by Sam's liquor-amplified snores.

Then George climbed through my window. (There was a route via the porch posts I'd showed him once.) He looked worried sick when I lit the candle on my nightstand. I showed him my beat-up legs.

I didn't tell him the other thing.

Much as I wished George would climb in beside me and hold me, for whatever his presence might have been worth in protection, I urged him to leave, terrified of what Sam might do if he caught a boy in my room. Not just any boy, either. The son and nephew of his two brand-new worst enemies. All I could think about was whether Mr. Graham and Uncle Jamie had any idea what danger they were in, that Sam was a killer.

After George left, I lay awake for ages, and when I finally did sleep at last, it was only fitfully. My legs hurt, and I kept remembering

Sam's invasive hand and the dirty, scared feeling just wouldn't go away.

(That's what started me off on wearing the long underwear all the time, even in the heat of summer. Especially after my body started changing. It complicates everything fashion-wise, but it also complicates matters for any disgusting person trying to stick their hands where they oughtn't.)

In the morning, I heard the car start and drive away, and immediately afterward my door scooched open a bit, making the legs of my bureau squeak against the floorboards.

"Louise!" Mother's voice said. "Get this thing away from the door this instant."

My mousy mother had *never* spoken to me with such sharp urgency in her voice before. It alarmed me. So I rolled off my bed, making faces because it hurt to do it, and pulled the bureau farther out of the way.

Mother pushed in. "Louise," she said again. She pulled my nightie off over my head and snatched up the nearest clean frock to hand, tugging it down over me as if she thought I'd forgotten how to dress myself. Then she snatched up a bag and began stuffing random things in it. "Don't wait another minute. You go straight to the Grahams' and do not come back until I tell you it's all right."

I opened my mouth to protest, but she shook her head, lips pressed to a thin white line in her whiter face. "Do not argue," she said. "He can't hurt me, but he can hurt you, and I've waited too long to get you out—"

The satchel fell to the floor and she dropped into my rocking chair, sobbing into her hands. I went to hug her but she pushed me away and said, "I'll be here to hug later. Go. Go quickly! You never know when he'll come back!"

I didn't take the satchel.

I just *ran*.

When I got to The Dump, George was just coming out of the barn with the milk and egg pails. I hugged him instead, praying that Sam wouldn't kill Mother in retaliation when he discovered I'd gone. That he wouldn't come storming over here to drag me back.

Here is a thing. I loved my mother. I still do and always will and I would DIE before letting anyone hurt her. But there are moments I am angry at her, too. For being so weak that she couldn't stand up for me BEFORE things got so bad. All the beatings and throwing stuff at me that Sam did—she just sat there and let it happen—and it had to come to THAT before she snapped out of her trance and into action?

I guess I should be glad anything at all woke her up, but she is a big reason why I want something different for myself when I grow up. Even if I get married and have babies, which I hope I will, I will stand up for them AND myself. I'll start by making sure I can take care of myself on my own, and after I'm sure of that I'll take the next step, which will be not marrying a jerk like Sam.

After George had got me inside The Dump, he rather rapidly declined into grouchiness, because I beelined for Uncle Jamie and his deerhounds the minute they all walked in, instead of (I suppose) devoting myself solely to George. We had breakfast, and I whispered to Uncle Jamie that I needed to talk to him and could we please go outside, somewhere where nobody could overhear?

George didn't follow, jealous little thing. We left him behind, sulking over his porridge, and walked into the trees, sat on a fallen log together while the dogs frolicked about, and I told him everything. Not just about the previous night, but about Daddy's murder, too, and all that came between. It was hard at first to know where to begin, but Uncle Jamie is very patient, and somehow I think he knew already what I was trying to say, and what questions he needed to ask to draw out my tale of woe.

He actually cried a little, something I've never seen a grown man do before. But then I remembered how the Bible says Jesus wept, so I thought maybe the world would be a better place if more men followed Jesus' example. Like *really* followed it, not just talked about it. Anyway, we looked into each other's eyes, and I saw something in Uncle Jamie's that made me know he really understood, and that he would stop at nothing now to protect me from further harm.

This is another reason I know he really understood: when he held out his hands to me, he asked me if it was all right to give me a hug. Of course it was, I thought at the time, but since then—especially after meeting those girls he and Aunt Estelle look after—I've wondered, how did he know I might not want some man touching me, even in a good way, after what Sam did? Did someone hurt him, too, once? Or someone he was close to? What made him so dedicated to helping as many vulnerable girls as he can fit into that beautiful little house he has for them?

Could you blame me for sticking to him like glue after that?

It's true that I did have some fun with George, making him think I had a crush on Uncle Jamie. Maybe I did, a bit, but only in an "I wish this man was my father" sort of way. (I can't be *completely* sure of this, but I think it may have also crossed my mother's mind that she wished he was my father too.) Anyway, that's how I have survived my entire life as the Pearson pariah: instead of letting (most) people see my fears or deepest feelings, like this new love for Uncle Jamie, I go all prickly or strange or downright ridiculous, just so people can't see the soft side of me.

If my soft side stays hidden, it can't get hurt.

George, bless his oblivious soul, didn't notice his dad passing Uncle Jamie his old service revolver—had no idea that, from that day forward, Uncle Jamie was with me constantly not because he preferred me, but because I needed a bodyguard, and this time he was prepared to truly disable Sam if he crossed our path and tried to make off with me again.

I don't know if Sam carried a gun. He was a criminal, but somehow I think a gun wouldn't have been his style. It was too loud and too honest a way to kill. But Uncle Jamie carrying one, plus the presence of his dogs, gave us a solid chance for a fair fight.

I've never told George any of this. He has no idea how much

danger I was really in, nor how scared I still am, even though Sam is dead, and I'd thought my reasons for fear were gone.

Because the implication of these filthy awful notes is that whoever is sending them would like to carry out Sam's threat to me.

And I am *tired*.

Tired of being a pawn for bad men against my mother.

We both deserve better, deserve to be free from all that, to have peace and safety.

But I'm still not convinced I'll ever deserve George.

June 12, 1927: Sunday

Mr. Charles Lindbergh has arrived back in the United States!

There was loads more about him in today's paper, AND a photograph of his plane, the *Spirit of St. Louis*, which I have carefully clipped out and added to the collection on my wall.

After lunch, George disappeared up to his room with the aura of someone who was Up to Something, and he wouldn't let me come in, so I pounded out all fifteen of Mother's variations of *Mary Had a Little Lamb*.

Very loudly.

Many times.

But instead of scolding me, the grownups melted away, leaving me all alone, which was boring. I'd hoped they'd try to distract me with something interesting.

But no.

So I gave up on Mary and her lamb to plop into the armchair to sulk.

There were other things I could have been doing, such as the stretches Mrs. Tabitha had assigned me to help me work up to doing the splits, or answering Uncle Jamie's latest letter, but it felt satisfyingly rebellious just sitting there, sitting.

That's where George found me when he finally emerged, hands behind his back, trying to look nonchalant. "Got something for you," he said, and I sat up, intrigued, all annoyance gone. "Shut your eyes."

I squeezed them shut and waited until I felt something smooth and flat come to rest on my knees. "Okay. Open them."

He'd been drawing me a picture, on a nice sturdy piece of cardboard. The airplane in it looked exactly like the one I'd clipped from the paper that morning, but he'd added an E at the end of "St. Louis", and standing near the plane he'd put Mr. Lindbergh himself.

But the part that made this picture really its own special brand of madness was that George had added me, lying on my stomach on the wing, planting a kiss on Mr. Lindbergh's cheek.

I looked up at George, beaming. "I love it," I said.

"You did wish that lady in France was you, didn't you?" he asked, color rising in his cheeks. *Silly adorable boy.*

"It did cross my mind," I said. Silently I added, *It's you I really want to kiss.* I jumped up and spun him around a few times, before we ran upstairs to my room to decide where to hang it.

I put it at the head of my bed, right beside Bessie Coleman, and then I said, "You really ought to sign it, don't you think?"

He went to his room for a pencil and wrote in the corner. *To Louise from George (the younger one). Wishful thinking?*

George and his mother are both so ridiculously good at so many things than nobody ever really taught them to do. Her with her cooking and rose-growing and being able to replicate anything from a fashion magazine, and him with his drawing and words and aptitude for languages. Whenever someone remarks on it—"is there ANYTHING you can't do?"—Mrs. Graham just waves it off with, "Well, I can't play the piano."

"You could learn," they say.

"I have to leave some things for other people to be better at than me," she'll reply, in a tone that gives no indication whether she's being flippant or serious.

Meanwhile, I'm good at math and Mother plays the piano, and those are good things, but it seems small in comparison with the genius that lives in George and his mother.

June 15, 1927: Wednesday

*L*ast night there was a moon eclipse. After we were supposed to be in bed, George and I went up through the attic onto the flat part of the roof, with a picnic basket and a lot of blankets and Lindbergh, and lay down to watch it.

The sky was beautifully clear and we got a perfect view. By the time we got up there, it was partially eclipsed already, but we'd had to wait until our parents were asleep, and it seemed to take them simply AGES to settle down and put their lights out.

George and Lindbergh were mostly interested in the picnic basket for the first twenty minutes or so. "I hope your mother wasn't planning to use that potato salad tomorrow," I remarked ominously as he devoured it.

"If she was, I'll make some more," he said, undisturbed. "What should I get Dad for Father's Day?"

"I saw a spectacularly ugly tie in Director's window a couple days ago. I bought it for him. You're on your own."

He laughed and set the empty dish back into the basket. "Well, you could still come along with me. You always have good ideas."

"Okay."

George lay down beside me and tossed open a blanket, under which Lindbergh promptly burrowed and curled up between us. George watched the moon in silence, and my mind drifted back to the last gift I'd given Daddy for Father's Day in 1924, when I was nine. I'd created it out of my stash of stray nuts and bolts, scraps of tin, some fishing line, and a few bent forks—things I'd picked up around the farm, like a magpie. The end result was a wind chime, of a sort. I painted BEST DAD on the top part. It was hideous, but I was so proud of it, and he was genuinely pleased. He hung it outside his and Mother's bedroom window, where the slightest breeze made a tinny tinkling sound.

I wonder what happened to it. We left Junction City in such a hurry, I have nothing left that belonged to Daddy except that sweater. Not one single other thing to remember him by that's mine. Mother has the portrait of the three of us hidden in her Bible, but that's hers.

It feels like he's fading. I can't remember the sound of his voice, and even his face I can't picture clearly, unless I sneak looks in Mother's Bible.

But I do remember how I felt when he was close by.

Safe.

Safe, like I felt right now, on this roof, with George and Lindbergh at my side, watching the earth's own shadow pass over the moon.

June 16, 1927: Thursday

*T*oday when George and I left the Crystal Gardens Ballroom after our lesson, there were two boys loitering across the street. I thought I recognized them from school, but I didn't know their names, and didn't give them another thought until I realized they were walking down the other side of the street, keeping pace with us, grinning with unsettling intensity. George had his nose in one of his library books and was trailing a few steps behind me, so I turned to hiss at him to hurry.

He looked up, saw the boys, and shut the book, stepping up to my side. When we reached the park in front of the capitol building, the one in the plaid shirt yelled out, "Hey! Ballet boy!"

George put his head down and kept walking.

"Ballet boy!" Plaid-Shirt's buddy with the newsie bow tie and suspenders jeered. His taunt caught the ears of some other lads who were tossing a ball nearby.

My blood was instantly up, and I couldn't decide which one I should punch first. Before I came to a conclusion, they'd all encircled us.

"Do you have to wear tights?" Plaid-Shirt asked with a smirk. "Bet Louise loves that. Olivia sure does."

"Bet you look cute in a tutu," said Newsie.

George kept his eyes on the ground, perfectly still. My hands balled into fists. Seeing it, Plaid-Shirt sniggered. "Ooooh, the dumb girl thinks she can fight."

"Maybe you can dance with Ballet Boy instead," Newsie said to Plaid-Shirt, and all of the boys guffawed. One of them began prancing with exaggerated daintiness, and Plaid-Shirt playfully shoved at him.

Prancer snatched at George's bag. George tried to grab it back, but he was too late. Prancer had already tossed it to Plaid-Shirt, who opened it and dumped it, scattering schoolbooks everywhere—and George's dance things. His face was becoming crimson as Newsie dangled an odd thing from his pinching fingers. It looked almost like underwear. "What's this then?"

He tossed it to Prancer, who dropped it onto his head like a hat. I flexed my hands, remembering that other time I'd punched out a boy, also in defense of George.

The problem with George is that he will just sit there and take this sort of thing until it gets out of hand, and I wasn't about to let it get out of hand. How had these boys found out, anyway, I wanted to know?

Stay angry, little one, you're going to need it.

None of them expected the Dumb Girl to pack the kind of punch she did. I grabbed Plaid-Shirt, socked him in the face, and swung around to Prancer and Newsie and knocked them down too. I felt like Samson in the Bible, slaying Philistines left and right with his stray jawbone-of-an-ass. "Anybody else?" I shouted, chest heaving, as the boys staggered back to their feet.

"Can't the ballet boy stick up for himself?" Prancer asked, trying to look mean through his blackening eye.

I just blacked his other eye. George, reactions now catching up at last with his look of blank horror, grabbed my arms and pinned them behind me. "Stop it, Louise!" he hissed. "You're not helping!"

"Let me go!" I wriggled furiously, but his grip was as strong as my punch.

An adult came striding over, calling out, "What's going on here?" and the bullies scattered, leaving us alone with the wreckage of George's bag strewn and trampled. George let go of my arms and I glared at him. "Ignoring them is not going to make them stop," I said.

"And you think beating them up is going to solve anything?"

The kind stranger helped us gather up the strewn items. He said he knew one of the boys and would be speaking to his parents about the incident, but aside from thanking him, George and I didn't speak the rest of the walk home. As soon as we were inside, George disappeared to his room, and I (still fuming) picked up the telephone receiver and asked for the Wisniewski residence.

As soon as I heard Olivia's voice I said, "How do boys from school know you like George in tights?"

There was dead silence on her end. Was it guilt or shock? At last she spoke. "I—I only told my friend Sandra about..." She hesitated. "That I like George."

I could practically hear her blushing as she whispered the words. "Who's Sandra?"

"My friend in school," she said. "Maybe she said something... but she promised to keep it a secret!" Olivia sounded near tears. "Don't say anything to George! Please?"

"He already knows," I said with a sigh. "I just punched three lads on our walk home for ganging up on us and calling him a sissy ballet boy and saying that you like him in tights."

"Oh, gosh," Olivia squeaked. "I'm so embarrassed."

"*And* they dumped out his bag and messed up all his stuff, so maybe don't say anything else to blabbermouth Sandra, because I'm tired of people torturing him." And I slammed down the phone.

JULY 1, 1927: FRIDAY

*T*hree things:

1. My mother can't cook, but she is good at making rooms
   beautiful
2. Olivia is very sorry about what happened
3. I will never get married in June

<u>My Mother Can't Cook But She Is Good At Making Rooms Beautiful</u>

I'm not sleeping on a pile of blankets anymore!

Not satisfied with merely papering the bedrooms, Mother convinced Mrs. Graham to go secondhand furniture shopping with her.

Now there are beds for Mother and me: a single with a trundle for her room, and a double for mine. Of course it's not my bed for keeps, and who knows who will have it when boarders live here, but it is so comfy and I am in love with it. And a set of two nightstands, so she and I each have one now.

Mother is having so much fun making the bedrooms come to life, combining just the right mismatched pieces to create comfortable, attractive spaces. She's hung translucent, snow-white muslin curtains in all the windows, and now she's busy braiding up long strips of rag from Mrs. Graham's rag bag to turn into rugs: blues and greys and golds for my room, pinks and whites and greens for the rose room.

Mrs. Graham is very pleased.

<u>Olivia Is Very Sorry About What Happened</u>

She came over after I slammed the phone down and we went into the back garden to sit by the roses and had a long talk while the hens kept us company. Olivia was deathly mortified that her confidence to Sandra was betrayed and she swears she'll never tell *her* any secrets ever again.

I looked up at George's open window. Lindbergh sat on the windowsill, yipping at us, wanting to come join us, but George didn't appear to let him down in his basket. It seemed odd he didn't.

Olivia interrupted my thoughts, still sniveling. "What did George say, when that boy said—what he said?"

"Nothing," I said. There was a long pause and I added, "What was that weird underwear thing, anyway?"

Olivia turned pink. "It's called a dance belt." At my blank stare, she explained in a squeaky whisper what it was for, and it was my turn to go hot in the face. Poor George.

(Although I wondered if Prancer might have had second thoughts about wearing it as a hat if he'd known where it had been not very long before.)

I decided to change the subject. "Anyway, you should know George isn't interested in girls at the moment, so if you're wanting

120

someone to be gooey with, you might want to look elsewhere." I rested my chin on my knees, sighing deeply.

Olivia's mouth dropped open. "You want him," she whispered. "Are you jealous, then?"

"I didn't say that."

"But it's true, isn't it?"

I sat up straight and said snappishly, "I didn't say anything like that, and I never will."

"Oh." she sank back against the fence, looking hurt, and I felt bad.

"Sorry," I said, more gently. "I'm just really upset about what happened, that's all."

"I know," she said, and laid a hand on my arm. We just sat in silence for a while before she stood up, saying she had to get home to supper, but she turned as she closed the gate to say, "My birthday's next week and Mama said I might ask some friends. Do you think you could come?

"I'll ask," I promised. "And ring you."

She smiled shyly, and skipped away down the sidewalk.

I Will Never Get Married in June

I don't EVER want to be counted among the "sixty-four couples who succumbed to the wiles of Cupid during the month of June".

First of all, it's just such a STUPID thing to say, and second of all "succumbed" sounds like they've all been struck down by some irreversible disease. Mrs. Graham laughed when I expressed my disgust.

"Don't marry a farmer, then."

"What has that to do with anything?" I asked. Mother's face had gone pink, so I felt sure the answer would be interesting.

"You're right it has absolutely nothing at all to do with Cupid," Mrs. Graham said. "It's purely practical. Get married in June and you're more likely to have your first baby between harvest and planting."

"How long does it take to make a baby?" I asked.

"Nine months."

I did some quick counting. "So next March Salem will be sixty-four babies richer?"

"Sixty-four babies who succumbed to gravity when the stork dropped them down the chimney," George said melodramatically, tossing the morning mail to the table near his father and resuming his own seat. "Not that the stork story is any more sensible than the Cupid one."

Mrs. Graham ignored his interjection and answered my question. "They might," she said. "Or they might not."

"What's that supposed to mean?"

"It means babies don't always come along as fast as that," Mrs. Graham said, buttering and marmalading a thick slice of toast. "Some people can't have children at all, and sometimes it takes years. Cecil and I were married for ages and never managed to have any."

"You just needed—" Mr. Graham began, but Mrs. Graham stuffed the toast in his mouth to shut him up.

"Enough of that, sir. Lydia looks like she wants to sink through the floor, poor thing. Is that a letter from Susan?"

Mother did look exactly like that. George studiously stuffed toast into his own mouth and pretended the conversation wasn't happening, while his father carefully slit open Susan's letter.

I leaned on the table and kept pushing. "But you and Mr. Graham didn't have to be married to have George, so why—"

Mr. Graham cut me off—whether because he hadn't heard me or to shut me up I was not sure—to exclaim, "Speaking of babies, guess what Susan has to say in this letter! 'Daddy darling, just guess what will be coming our way in September! I didn't say anything sooner because there was a little trouble to start with and I wanted to be sure. Robert is convinced there are two in there, so be prepared, GRANDPAPA.'"

(The idea of Mr. Graham as a grandfather is incredibly strange. He doesn't seem old enough.)

But he was clearly over the moon, and dashed off a letter immediately before having to rush away to work, leaving it for George to address and send. We took Lindbergh with us on our walk to drop it at the post office, and I said, "It took Susan a lot longer than nine months."

George rolled his eyes.

"And mine were married in June and I didn't come along 'til September."

"The way mine carry on you'd think there'd have been a lot more than just me," George said, sounding unimpressed.

"I never saw mine do anything like yours."

He muttered something that sounded very much like *What a pity we can't swap.*

July 10, 1927: Sunday

*T*oday was my confirmation day.

I'd already almost completed my classes at my Turner church, so Reverend Tully came over a couple of times to finish them off. It would have been nice to do it at Easter like the rest of the kids, but it also was sort of fun to be The Special One. I wore my white dress from Aunt Estelle, the one she had made for me to wear to the big farewell party at the castle last summer (with a nice big hem that Mrs. Graham let down for me!) She also made me a sort of crown out of the roses on her beloved white rose bush, with some leftover green chiffon, and another bunch to pin at the shoulder of my dress. It was so elegant and I felt very grown up. She even helped me with my hair! I spent all of yesterday with it rolled up in a row of little buns pinned in place, and it actually sort of worked and I had a little bit of wave and I am very excited about it. Mr. Graham took a picture of me in front of the rose bushes before we all left for the service and I hope it comes out.

He and Mrs. Graham surprised me by coming too—he in the appalling tie I gave him for Father's Day. Mother wore a new dress that Mrs. Graham made her: pale green silk and chiffon, with pink chiffon roses at the waist. It's the first truly pretty dress I can remember Mother having. I know she had a beautiful dress for her wedding, which she says was navy blue taffeta, but of course I can't ever remember her wearing it afterwards, and I don't even know if she kept it. I certainly haven't ever seen it. Anyway, she also wore the pearl earrings that she doesn't often bring out.

(Not all Presbyterian kids have confirmations, but for my Lutheran-raised mother, it is a very important rite of passage, and she insisted.)

I won't write about the entire ceremony, because if you really want to know all that is said, you can flip open the 1921 *Book of Common Worship* to page 47 and read it for yourself. (I know this because George has a copy, which I am sure will come as an utter shock.)

George helped me choose the Bible verse to use on the little cards I had printed out to give all my friends, too. That was Mother's idea, and we went to a printer and had them make them. I wanted something about flying, and George suggested Isaiah 40:30 and 31, and then we added my name and the date. I got a dozen. I already gave away one each to Mother and George and Mr. and Mrs. G, so I have enough to give one to Mrs. T and each of her girls and Opal and Margie too, and of course I'll send one to Uncle Jamie next time I write him. And Mother gave me a lovely new Bible all my own, too.

After lunch, George and I lay out back in the grass, surrounded by Lindbergh and the trio of hens. Krumbles was sitting on George's chest, facing off her canine rival, who thought he ought to be there. "When are you going to decide about getting baptized?" I asked him. (George, not Lindbergh.)

"I'm still working through it."

"How so?"

His fingertips lightly stroked Krumbles' feathers. "Well, I've been thinking lately about how Jesus' disciples didn't stop being Jewish just because they followed him and believed He was Messiah, any more than Dad will ever stop being Scottish just because he lives in America—"

"He is a citizen now, though," I said. "Why does it matter, anyway?"

"For one thing, I'll never stop being Jewish in the sense that I was born Jewish. People who hate Jews won't care if I practice

126

Christianity, because of who my mother is. Just because I can hide behind my father's name if I want to... well, I am who I am, and I'll always know." Krumbles flapped furiously at Lindbergh and walked off, and Lindbergh bounced onto George and slurped at his face before settling down to look at Krumbles with a triumphant doggy smile. "If I had a name like Cohen or Rosenthal or something like that..." he trailed off, and for a time he was silent.

Then he launched into a long and systematic exposition about the Continuity of the Thread of Scripture, how the Old and New Testaments are all one story, and being Jewish but also believing Jesus was the Messiah could add a depth of understanding many Christians overlook.

Or something. I admit I stopped listening after a while. I guess I'm more practical about my faith, whereas George is more cerebral about his, and that's okay.

But the reason I stopped listening wasn't because he was boring. His enthusiasm about these things is infectious, even if I don't always understand what he's trying to say. It was because, as I watched him, squinting in the sunshine, talking with his hands, and being walked all over by his rambunctious puppy and preaching with such earnestness—well—

In those moments I felt I lived my entire life, saw my entire future, like one of Cousin Thomas' ants trapped in amber for eternity: me, with George, forever. Him being earnestly theological, and me being there to keep him from descending into dusty dullness, and it was *perfect*.

It was as if someone said out loud in my ear: *You might as well get used to this, because this is your future.*

It *might* have been wishful thinking.

But it's also when I first realized that what I felt for George wasn't just a curious crush or passing fancy. I *was* going to marry him, and we were going to be together forever. This feeling of devotion startled me, made me feel stupidly shy all of a sudden, in case he would see it in my face. (AS IF.) He was too busy expounding to notice, and I was too busy admiring to hear.

I wondered whether, under the shyness he displayed regarding romance, he'd ever thought of me this way. If he ever will realize the same thing I just did, and ask me to marry him so we can love each other especially forever.

I guess if he doesn't I'll have my plane for company, but surely he will soon change his mind about romance. Olivia has boys in her class chasing her, and she's a grade behind us!

Or maybe George just has an unusual way of showing love. Because I'm learning everyone does that a little differently, and it doesn't make it any less real for all that.

My father's way was by taking care of Mother and me, protecting us from the Bad Pearsons. Mother's is teaching me to play the piano because it's the only thing she seems to be really proud of in her life.

Mr. Graham's way is by affectionate touches and hugs and making terrible jokes. Mrs. Graham's way is by feeding everybody in her path with delicious food.

I haven't been able to figure out what George's way is, though. I don't think "reading aloud to Louise" counts because he's so darned pleased with himself about his own oratory talents that I'm not sure it's really about me at all, in the end.

I know the way I like to be loved: being cuddled. Daddy used to, before he died: let me snuggle up on his lap while he read me my bedtime stories. Mother's never done that, not since I was very small. I wish she would. Maybe she thinks I'm too old for that now. I'm not sure how to tell her I will never be too old for hugs.

And George, although he's not as averse as his mother to being touched, doesn't seem keen on volunteering anything beyond the casual, and I've had it drilled into me that girls aren't supposed to make the first move when it comes to romantic gestures.

I guess I'll have to make do with what touching I get dancing with him.

Which isn't much at lessons because we're still such beginners and have so much to learn before partnering.

But there's always the foxtrot.

*T*oday the five of us plus dog climbed into the Buick and went to the coast to get away from the hot city a bit. Destination: Lincoln City!

I spent my first nine years in Junction City, which is flat farmland. Turner and Salem are still in the same valley, and although they certainly have more trees than Junction City, I had no idea that, so close to home, there are these GORGEOUS THICKLY-WOODED HILLS between us and the coast. More trees in one place than I have ever seen!! With cattle feeding in fields here and there!

It was a long and twisty ride, and it made Mother rather carsick, and George was too busy reading a Hebrew something-or-other to notice anything else, and Lindbergh was bouncing around like a rubber ball, but I loved the drive. Mr. Graham regaled us with

Scottish airs he spontaneously made up new words for every time he saw something interesting he wanted to announce to us in song.

You'll take the back seat
And I'll take the front seat,
And I'll be at the ocean afore ye...

In the dried-up brittle field
Eat the little grass it yields
For water you've appealed
Bonnie cattle, O!

And it's no, nay, never,
No, nay never no more;
Will I tame this wild terrier?
No never no more...

Mrs. Graham, rolling her eyes at him, swapped seats with Mother about halfway there so Mother would feel less sick and Mrs. Graham could attempt to nap. She snuggled herself up into the corner opposite George (interestingly, also as far as possible from her operatic husband). This left me in the middle seat, a Convenient and Useful Barrier between Mrs. Graham and the Behated Dog. (Why isn't *behated* the opposite of *beloved*? Because it should be.) Of course Lindbergh spent half the trip sitting on the back of Mr. Graham's seat, licking his face, or trying to get in the way of his feet.

When we arrived at the beach house the Grahams had rented, we took in our bags. Mrs. Graham inspected the cupboards and made a list of things to go shopping for. Since Mr. G was the only (legal) driver in our party, the adults left George and Lindbergh and me to our own devices while they went to the shops, and we decided to walk out onto the beach. George clipped on Lindbergh's leash so he wouldn't run off, and we set out.

There were plenty of other folks there, but there was so much lightness in my heart, knowing that my note-leaving creep couldn't possibly know where I was right now, and I allowed myself to be as exuberant as the ecstatic puppy, screaming with delight as I raced breakers with him and George. It had been over two months since the last note, after all. Maybe whoever it was had given up.

When the adults found us, our mothers sedately spread a blanket on the sand to sit and knit on while they watched us, but Mr. Graham took off his shoes and socks and joined us in being ridiculous. (He really is rather like an overgrown child sometimes.) Anyway, we were all starving by the time we headed back to the cottage for supper. Mr. Graham was required to thoroughly bathe and dry "that animal" before he was reluctantly allowed to set foot in the cottage. George, volunteering to cook, smirked that at least where rented homes were concerned, his mother was less particular about Lindbergh being indoors.

George made us tinned soup (which he did not burn) and sandwiches that were like grilled cheese except he dipped them in some eggy stuff after the cheese got melty and fried them again. I said they were better than the Dempster Dilly Dream, and he said he didn't agree, but dill would have been a wonderful addition to the eggy stuff and next time he'd add some.

"You do realize not *everything* has to be dill-flavored, right?" I said.

He looked at me as if I'd turned into a monster. "Do you not like dill?" he asked, the soup ladle raised vaguely weapon-like in his hand.

"In moderation," I said. "But it doesn't have to be on everything."

"Dill is like salt," his mother interjected. "What good is a dish without dill?"

"Do not argue with the Russian element of this family," Mr. Graham murmured from the table where he was slicing each sandwich in half diagonally. "You will never win. Anyway, there's no dill in the empire biscuits!"

The prospect of Mrs. Graham's famous jammy shortbread was enough to stop the war before it began, and we sat down to enjoy our tomato soup (without dill) and eggy cheese sandwiches (also without dill).

It was a marvelous week-end. On Saturday we explored the beach and all the shops, stuffing ourselves with saltwater taffy and ice creams and bought kites and fresh fish that Mrs. Graham fried for lunch (the fish, not the kites), with some dill that mysteriously materialized in the cottage kitchen, and spent the afternoon flying the new kites. Even our mothers took turns with them.

On Sunday the three of us who cared found a church to go to, while the two of us who didn't disappeared somewhere and didn't show up again until long after the three of us who did had returned from church and finished our lunch ("jacket potatoes", with cheese and broccoli and beans.) They both looked rather pleased with themselves when they did eventually show up and found us on the beach.

Bet they were off somewhere KISSING.

(All I know is that *I* was off nowhere kissing.)

Anyway, we had a fantastic time, building a sandy replica of Inverlochy Castle and its gardens in between running into the water. (Mr. Graham, having grown up with the sea at his back door, is an expert at making sand castles!) We came back to the cottage Extremely Drenched and Sandy, and all of us had to hose off outside to keep from tracking half the beach indoors, then took turns having baths before lounging around the sitting room, eating apples and copious amounts of popcorn while the wireless played music George and I could dance to, and then we all played Twenty-One as best we could with Lindbergh constantly trying to eat the discard pile.

July 25, 1927: Monday

I AM FURIOUS.

Of all the weekends Mr. Graham had to choose for a beach getaway, he chose the ONE WEEKEND THERE WERE AIRPLANE RIDES AT THE FAIRGROUNDS.

Not that it's really his fault; he tried to reserve that cottage ages ago and this past weekend was the first it was available.

But still.

AIRPLANE RIDES.

We got home around noon on Monday, and Mr. Graham went straight to the office to check in on things, and George perused the pile of newspapers that had stacked up, so he's the one that found the ad. At dance that afternoon, Margie said she and her big brother had a ride. It was $3.50 per person, but the Waco (that's the type of plane it was) has room for two extra people besides the pilot, so they're making more per ride than the $5 rides usually go for. A clever racket! I have $8 saved up. I'd have paid for both seats so I could ride alone, IF I HAD HAD THE CHANCE.

Mr. Graul, the pilot giving the rides, is also a flight instructor. Oh, however did I get so terribly unlucky?

"What was it like?" I asked Margie, as we all were changing back into our street clothes after the lesson.

"It was windy," she said. "But fun. My brother was able to see our house, real tiny!"

"Why do you want to ride a plane so much?" Olivia asked me as she re-tied the ribbon in her hair.

"I'm going to fly planes someday," I said.

"Oh." She buttoned up the front of her frock and stuffed her dance things into her bag, slinging it over her shoulder. "I want to get married and have babies instead."

"I'm going to do that too. Both."

"But girls can't do both!" she protested.

"This one can." I explained to her then how fathers manage to be fathers and still work at jobs and do things they love. "Mothers are people too! They shouldn't have to give up everything they like doing, just to have babies for the sake of having babies!"

Opal, Olivia, and Margie all stared at me wide-eyed at this radical and wicked-sounding concept. I couldn't tell if it was alarm or enlightenment in their expressions.

I hoped it was the latter.

July 29, 1927: Friday

Colonel Lindbergh's book, *We*, just released a couple days ago. I saw a copy in the bookshop today when George and Lindbergh and I went to buy our weight in peppermint sticks. Okay, only two pounds actually, but they were having a sale on broken pieces, and it was only thirty cents for those two pounds. We split them carefully when we got home, using Mrs. Graham's kitchen scale, and I gave George fifteen cents out of my precious airplane fund.

It was worth it.

Usually I don't want books, but I want *We*. I couldn't bring myself to spend more of my hard-earned money on a book, though.

After the division of the peppermint sticks, we each took a couple and went out back with Lindbergh to work on teaching him to come when called. George worked with the dog, that is. I flopped onto one of the chairs, lounging in a very unladylike sprawl as I held my peppermint stick between my fingers as if it was a cigarette, sucking the end into a dagger-sharp point. Daddy used to always put a giant peppermint stick into my Christmas stocking every year, so I associate the taste with cold, wet winter.

If I closed my eyes, inhaling the sharp mintiness, I could imagine I was a snow princess with a sledge pulled by a team of adorably puffy arctic foxes, glamorously smoking as my polar subjects cheered with silver bells, and I languidly tossed my extra red-and-white-striped fairyland cigarettes to them as I passed. They didn't know my secret, that the princess they saw was actually a very angry dragon, and if anyone managed to steal the crown off my head, I would return to my natural form and melt all the ice on the pole and my subjects would meet a watery doom. For some time, lost in this reverie, I almost forgot the actual heat, but then Lindbergh leapt up on my lap hoping for a peppermint of his own, and I groaned, pushing him off. "It's SO HOT."

And George said, "Well, nobody's forcing you to wear wooly sweaters and long underwear in July, are they?"

It was sarcasm, of course, but it felt like a stab. Margie had asked why I always wore them, but George, the Boy Who Notices Nothing, had noticed too, and I felt sudden, intense self-loathing. My too-big sweaters, my protective armor, my concealers of shame. I squeezed my eyes shut, holding completely still, the contents of the threatening notes all flashing before my mind's eyes, the feel of Sam's disgusting hand. I willed myself not to cry. There is so much George doesn't know, so much I simply cannot tell him

George had continued past me after his remark, but he turned to see me frozen in place behind him and I forced out some words.

"It's not your concern about the long underwear."

"I didn't mean—" Now he was turning pink at the ears. I knew he thought I was offended that he'd mentioned the word *underwear*. We weren't the same carefree ten-year-olds anymore who'd shamelessly run around The Dump in our combinations. "Sorry, Lou, you're right. It's not my business."

I dropped my unfinished fairyland cigarette/stripey dagger to the ground and went inside without replying, and came up here to my room to write it out, hoping it would make me feel better. I guess it sort of has. I think maybe now I'll write a letter to Uncle Jamie.

Since he's the only person I don't have to hold anything back from, I think I'm going to tell him about the notes.

I just got out my confirmation cards to put one in the envelope with my letter, and the count isn't coming up right. I've given away nine, and I should have three left, but there was only one in my nightstand drawer, and it was pushed back out of sight.

I went down to where the adults were and asked if they knew what had happened to the other two, but they didn't. "Did you take them anywhere with you? Might you have dropped them accidentally?" Mother asked.

I had taken them to dance class the week of my confirmation, but I was positive all three were still in the printer's envelope when I brought them home. I couldn't remember checking, though, so it was possible they'd fallen out.

With a huge sigh, I went back up to address and stamp the letter, kissing the lone last card as I tucked it in. I'd wanted to keep one for myself, but now I wouldn't be able to.

AUGUST 7, 1927: SUNDAY

"You've never lived till you've flown!"

That is something Bessie Coleman said, and today I found out she was completely correct.

I am no longer furious at Mr. Graham for taking us to the coast that other weekend, because Mr. Graul and his glorious Waco were back today, AND

I HAD A RIDE IN THAT WACO

I am BURSTING with it.

I don't know where to start. I guess with the newspaper, because this morning George came in after his paper route was done and, in spite of his constant harping about how dangerous planes are, he looked incredibly smug as he unfolded it onto the breakfast table and framed his hands around the part he knew I'd want to see.

"And there's a whole article about how Mr. Graul's going to teach flying here with someone named Rankin," he went on. "I'll read it to you."

I think maybe he is still trying to make it up to me about the underwear comment.

I was so busy staring at that glorious item, and so excited, that I couldn't even be bothered to eat breakfast (porridge with honey and fresh blueberries) and George asked, "Are you going to eat that?" after I'd left it untouched for thirty-odd seconds. I pushed the bowl towards him and floated up the stairs, opening my pocketbook to count and recount my money. Twenty-five cents for the offering plate at church would still leave me with seven dollars and fifteen cents. I could pay for both seats and have that ride all to myself, as I so desperately longed to do. Twenty-eight hours' worth of entertaining noisy small people for a glorious few minutes in the air? Worth it. Absolutely worth it.

It had to be.

I ran a comb through my hair and put on the first dress I took out, topped it with one of my "frightful cardigans" (Mother's words) (it wasn't Daddy's, but it was still too big) and smacked into George running out of my room.

"Sorry," I said. He had his tie in his hand, and I took it and had it done up in a jiff.

"How'd you get so good at that, anyway?" he asked, inspecting himself in the bathroom mirror. His voice sounded echoey. I leaned on the doorframe, watching him make minute rearrangements to his hair with his fingers.

"Daddy," I said. "He was missing a finger on one hand. I don't remember it happening so I must have been a baby or not born yet... and he had trouble with tying things, so I learned how and did it for him. He only wore ties on Sundays and to town or to special things like school programs. He wasn't all Mr. Posh like you."

"I couldn't care less," George's echoey voice came again. "Dad's the posh one. And you, apparently." He emerged and fetched his Bible out of his room and slipped into his shoes (the kind without laces, because he's hopeless) and went ahead of me down the stairs, allowing

me to covertly admire him.

The ballet lessons are paying off, I think. He moves so much more gracefully than any other boy at school. He grouses about being shorter than I am, but the way he carries himself makes him seem taller than he is.

Also, I think the melodrama of balletic gestures appeals to the part of his heart that is all about performing. Just this past week he's taken to skidding into a room and doing the Spread-Your-Arms-Out-Palms-Up Thing to accompany THE MOST inane statements.

"I believe I shall go to Dempster's for a sandwich."

"What a fetching tie you have, my father!"

"When do we eat?"

"Daisy Delight is on the telephone for you."

"The sun is in the sky!"

"My very good dog will cause no trouble if you allow him into your house!"

Anyway, enough mooning over the boy who will never have it occur to him to add, "Louise, might I bestow a kiss upon your longing lips?" to the above list of statements.

As on Lindbergh Sunday, my mind wasn't on church at all. It was entirely taken up by the thought that sometime this very day I could climb into an airplane and take off.

George had to poke me out of my reverie when it was time to go, I was that lost in my happy dream. Mother had finished her postlude on the organ, so even she was waiting for me. And then we had to walk home, and then we had to eat lunch, and then we had to wait for Mr. Graham to be ready, which took approximately FOREVER, because grownups never seem to be in a hurry about anything IMPORTANT, like MAKING SURE LOUISE GETS TO THE FAIRGROUNDS BEFORE MR. GRAUL IS DONE GIVING RIDES FOR THE DAY.

"I could drive myself!" I loudly shouted to nobody in particular, from the little bench by the front door where I'd been waiting.

(And waiting.)

"No," Mother's voice came, equally loudly, from some unseen place.

Wetblanket.

"He won't be done giving rides for ages," George said, appearing around the corner. He'd slung a knapsack over one shoulder and went outside with Lindbergh's leash in hand. I followed him, watching him chase down the dog to attach the leash.

"You don't KNOW he won't be done," I countered.

The passenger seat of the car was rather furred from Lindbergh using it as a napping spot, so George spent several minutes using the comb from his pocket to gently scrape it off while I bounced from foot to foot, waiting. "Maybe he'll run out of fuel and have to stop before we get there!"

"I'm sure he's prepared for that extremity," Mr. Graham said, appearing AT LAST. He fired up the car. "Do you really suppose the entire town is queued up for aeroplane rides, Louise?"

"Probably you'll only be the fifth person to 'queue up'," George said. "And he'll be bored stiff waiting for anyone to come along, and then you'll descend on him like a whirlwind and he'll wonder what in the world just hit him..."

We passed the bookshop and I blew a kiss to *We*, still prominent in the window display. George didn't notice; he was sprawled out over the entire back seat with one hand keeping Lindbergh from vaulting out the window at exciting smells, and the other holding some new boring-looking library book that was about three inches thick and full of unpronounceable names. Mr. Graham started in on one of his spontaneous parodies again.

144

If a pilot meets a pilot
Comin' through the sky...

(He's ridiculous.)

When we reached the fairgrounds and parked, I bounced nearly as much as Lindbergh. His doorstop novel safely stowed back into his knapsack, George was too occupied trying to keep his dog out of trouble to pay much mind to me.

The Waco was just coming in for a landing. I stood there, staring, until it came to a full stop, and then I set off running as fast as I could go. Lindbergh caused a delay when he found a beautiful patch of dust to roll around in and refused to go anywhere until he'd become thoroughly dust-colored. George was almost as dusty and extremely put out by the time he'd caught me up, Lindbergh tucked firmly under his arm like a naughty monkey, and Mr. Graham at his heels trying very hard not to laugh.

"Hurry up," I called, and kept running until I'd reached the plane.

It's not very big, a Waco, not really. That surprised me a little.

I know how flight works and why planes lift into the air, but this was my first time seeing one in the flesh. Or... in the metal, I suppose? It looked so very, very *solid*, sitting there on the ground waiting for its next passengers.

Mr. Graham steered me into line, murmuring something about Americans not knowing how to queue to save their lives. George set Lindbergh down, and the puppy promptly wound his leash around his master's legs, then whined piteously because he couldn't keep circling. George also looked at the plane and said, "How in the world can that even get into the air?"

I shouted a lecture about the four principles of flight over the noise of the engine, to which he probably wasn't listening, all the while keeping my eyes glued to the plane as it rolled down the field and lifted into the air. The silence it left behind was a sad silence, and I anxiously followed the flight with my eyes. It was hard to see for a while, against the afternoon sun.

"Aren't you even a *little* afraid?" George asked.

"No," I said.

I got to watch it land and take off twice before it was my turn. I went straight up to the pilot, held out my hand, and said:

"My name is Louise Pearson and I have worked twenty-eight hours watching rambunctious small people to earn the money for this ride, and I will pay for both seats so I can go up by myself, and please don't say no."

Mr. Graul gave me a funny look. "You have a parent here, kid?"

"Dad is here," George said, unfurling a hand toward Mr. Graham, who waved and gave a thumbs up.

Before Mr. Graul could speak again, I went on. "I'm going to fly planes as soon as I'm old enough. This is the closest I've gotten to a plane so far. May I touch it?"

"Go ahead," he said, and I reverently laid my fingers against the fuselage.

"If I stay around until you're done giving rides, may I look at the engine too? What kind of engine is it?"

For the next five minutes I fired intelligent questions at him, the same way I'd done with Mr. Ball at his garage in Turner before I took the Buick's engine apart last winter, and Mr. Graul seemed to catch on quickly that I wasn't just any kid, I really cared. He saw that I actually knew what I was talking about, and that I understood his answers.

"Your brother doesn't want to go along?" Mr. Graul asked, nodding towards George as I held out my seven dollars.

"He's not my brother," I said at the same time George said, "I wouldn't ride in that thing for seventy times seven." (Which didn't make any sense, but that's George for you.) Lindbergh bounced, and Mr. Graham took his leash so he could have a nice gambol where there were fewer people to tangle up with, and left George to look after me.

"Not many girls want to fly planes," Mr. Graul said.

"Plenty want to."

"How old are you?"

"I'll be thirteen next month."

"Thirteen." He mused. "I've got a fourteen year old boy I've been training, and he's doing well. Didn't start out knowing half so much as you seem to, either."

146

I beamed at him. "More girls would fly planes, if only people wouldn't tell them they can't or shouldn't. Or if the girls just knew better than to believe that rubbish."

His eyes twinkled. "Anyone told you you can't or shouldn't?"

"Lots of shouldn't. Nobody would dare tell me can't. I taught myself to drive our car last winter after I took apart the engine and put it all back together again."

Mr. Graul threw back his head and laughed.

"Anyway, the air is where I belong. I've known it for two years. It calls me. Harriet Quimby and Bessie Coleman are my heroines."

Mr. Graul studied me hard for a few minutes, then he said, "Listen, there's nobody waiting after you just now. I'll take you up for half an hour, if you promise to keep it under your hat."

"Would you really?" I clasped my hands under my chin. I couldn't stop smiling.

"Yep." He gave me a conspiratorial wink.

I went through the motions of sealing my lips, and he handed me his extra leather flying helmet, which I strapped on, grinning at George like the Cheshire Cat. Mr. Graham snapped a photograph.

George was leaning his back against the fence. Freed of the responsibility of the bouncy puppy for the moment, he had his book open, but he wasn't reading it, just watching me. He didn't smile.

"Come along up." Mr. Graul held out his hand to help me step onto the wing and into the front seat. I was thankful for the long underwear, despite it being too warm, because it prevented the entire field getting a peep show at my pants.

Mr. Graul strapped me in, telling me what everything was (rudder, throttle, and so forth) and what not to touch (any of it). He climbed into the seat behind, and his friend Mr. Rankin on the ground swung the propeller for him. I closed my eyes and let the noisy vibration of the engine fill me, inhaling the invigorating scents of fuel and oil and warm metal. I listened to the subtle changes in the voice of the engine as Mr. Graul taxied to the place he started each takeoff. Then I opened my eyes, because I really didn't want to miss a thing.

For a fleeting second I wished Mr. Graul was flying from my seat so I could watch what he was doing from behind, but just as quickly

I knew I would completely miss the point of this experience if I did that, so I just relaxed and prepared to enjoy the view.

I waved at George as we sped past him, his book still open and unread, for once holding less attraction to him than me.

And he looked worried. Genuinely terrified. And my heart twisted a little and I thought, *He's afraid of all those news items about crackups because he's afraid for ME.* I didn't have time to process that lovely idea, however, as now we were gathering more speed and then, abruptly, became weightless.

I leaned over the edge as far as I could and watched the shadow of the plane undulating along the ground as it fell away beneath us: a shadow from the sky. The outline of something real that wasn't actually real in itself. Not only the plane cast a shadow, but the trees, too, slanting out long in the late afternoon sun. Even the sparse, fluffy clouds in the west cast shadows. I never thought of clouds having shadows.

They had no substance, those shadows, not in themselves, but they made what was real somehow clearer, put things into perspective in ways you'd never perceive them from ground level. As if by stepping back from one's small, narrow world, a whole new one can open up.

The cold wind on my face made it hard to breathe, but I was ecstatic. I wasn't really alone up here, not with Mr. Graul at the controls behind me, but since I couldn't see him, I felt like I owned the entire sky, and the clouds, and the shadows. I stretched out my arms on either side of me, wishing I could take it all into my embrace and shout to it all how much I loved it. Instead I just screamed, "I'M FLYING!!" over and over into the wind, which whipped my voice away and left my throat hoarse.

The half hour was over long before I was ready, and yet it also was the longest half hour of my life. Time is funny that way. When we'd landed and Mr. Graul cut the engine, Mr. Graham and George (Lindbergh in his arms again) came to meet us. "You look as if you just saw the face of God," Mr. Graham said, a soft fondness in his eyes. For just one brief moment, he reminded me of Uncle Jamie.

"I feel like I did," I said. "I wish I could have stayed up there forever."

148

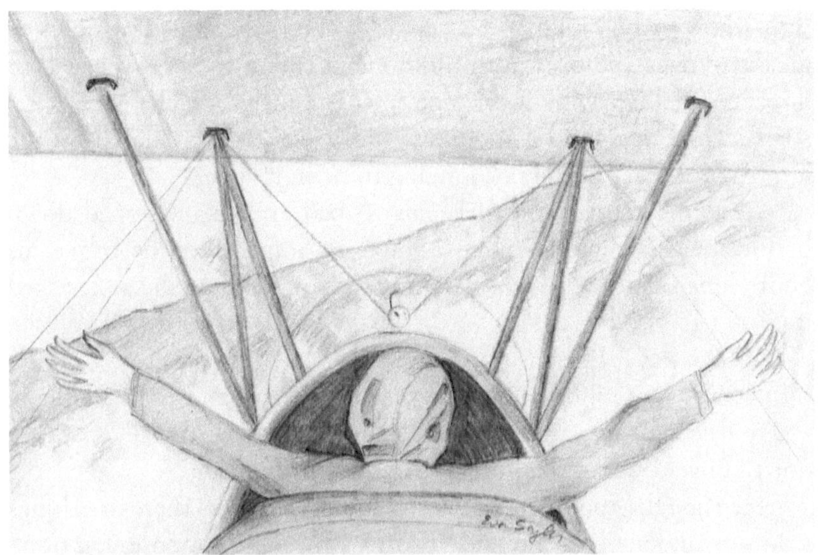

George didn't say a word, only seemed relieved that I was still alive and in one piece. And then they waited while I talked Mr. Rankin's and Mr. Graul's ears off. And waited. And waited.

(What can I say, they made ME wait when I was ready to come earlier?)

We took a long, roundabout way home after. Mr. Graham hummed softly to himself, unusually restrained in his chatter. George petted Lindbergh and didn't say anything or try to read his book. I hardly noticed any of them.

I devoured several cream cheese and cucumber sandwiches upon our return. (Mother is capable of making sandwiches. You can't burn those.) And Mrs. Graham had made a trifle with strawberries and blueberries, chocolate sauce, whipped cream, and vanilla cake, which was delicious.

Afterwards, George and I sat in the grass in the back garden with Lindbergh and the hens, while from out an open window the sound of Mother's piano playing drifted out to us through the dusk. It was Beethoven's 29th piano sonata, which she'd been practicing for days in her quest to add all his sonatas to her repertoire. She still had three to go.

(The thing nobody ever tells you about living with a musician is just how much of what you hear at home is the same few notes or measures over and over again millions of times, so I was relieved to hear her finally playing it through start to finish for a change.)

I sighed, too full of happiness for words, and lay down on the lumpy grass, eyes to the sky, longing to be in it again.

George got up to put his hens to bed and then flopped down beside me, his shoulder almost touching mine. Then he broke his hours-long silence with one question, his voice almost shy as he asked it.

"What was it like?"

"It was like... like being stuck in quicksand and then suddenly you're free. Not just free. You're suspended *and* soaring, all at once. I don't know how to explain it. You're the word person."

He thought about that a while. "I guess—I guess there are things I do not understand," he said at last. "I mean—I suppose you don't probably understand why I want to be a minister, either."

"It will be a fantastic way for you to talk all the time and feel unashamed for never shutting up," I said, grinning. He punched my arm lightly and we both laughed.

"No, I mean—" He paused. "I saw your face when you came out of the plane. I don't understand what it is that draws you to risking your neck in one of those things, but I guess I don't have to understand, just accept that you know better than anyone else what you're meant to do."

"Thanks," I said softly. "I hoped you'd come to realize that." After a minute I went on, "And I do think I understand you too. You want to use your gifts for good—your voice, your way with words—it could help people. Teach them. I don't have that. All I have is a brain full of numbers and navigation and engines. It's a bit hard being a girl when that's all you've got. If you don't want to be trapped, I mean."

"I suppose so." He reached out to Lindbergh to scratch his head absentmindedly. "Do you think being married is a trap, then?"

My heart caught and fluttered, not daring to hope that George was developing feelings that mirrored my own for him, and I formed my response carefully. "It's only a trap if you don't have a way out. A way to still be you. Like... look at my mother. She has no skills."

"She plays piano and she's a cracking interior decorator."

"But I don't know if she could make a living off those things," I said. "She's spent all her adult life up to recently stuck on a farm where everyone hated her. She can't drive a car and the only reason we've been okay since Sam died is because for months she'd been squirreling away the money he kept giving her to keep quiet. It's not going to last forever. She doesn't own the house in Turner and eventually we'd have had to leave. People just took pity on us, I guess. But my point is that, she'll have to find some other man to marry if she doesn't find a way to support herself soon, and it's unfair that she should have to risk being stuck to another awful man just so she can eat and have a roof over her head, see?"

He thought about that. "So you mean you want to be able to take care of yourself in the event you're ever left alone for any reason, is that it?"

"Yes." *He understood.* "And any children I might have. I do want to have a family someday. I just... I never want to depend so much on a man that I have nothing to fall back on."

Lindbergh flopped into the narrow space of grass between us, making George laugh. He propped himself up on one elbow, and I looked at him and he looked at me, with a few stars and the rising sliver of moon in the sky behind his head, and I held my breath. This was a *perfectly* swoon-worthy moment for a first kiss. And he did have this sort of dreamy look in his eyes, so it was a perfectly reasonable assumption on my part, and goodness knows I was absolutely dying for him to kiss me. What a perfect ending that would be to this perfect day!

And he said:

"I wonder if there is any trifle left."

I guess I shall just have to die unkissed.

I left George to demolish the remnants of trifle and curled up in my bed, head still too blissfully full of sky to even mind so terribly much about Not Being Kissed, remembering the wind in my face, until I fell asleep to dream of stars.

I would name my plane after a star.

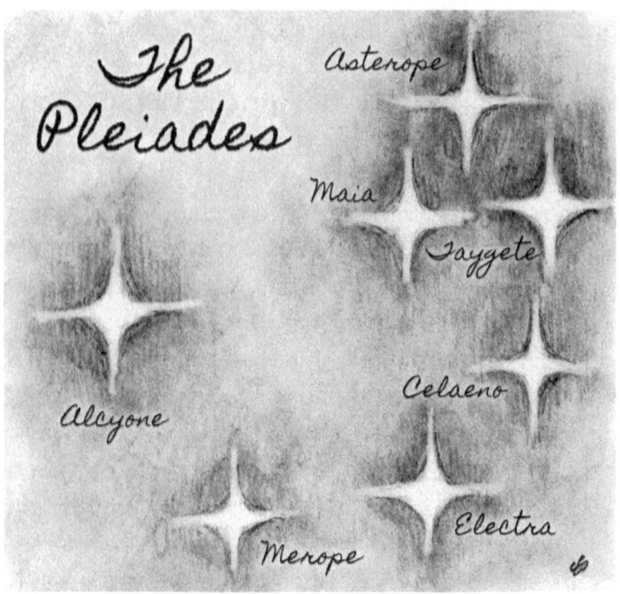

One of the Pleiades, perhaps. The seven sisters from Greek mythology Uncle Jamie told me about last summer on a very clear night, when several of us went up to one of the castle turrets to stargaze. Maia, Electra, Taygete, Alcyone, Celaeno, Merope, Asterope—those were the names of the seven sisters, supposedly turned into stars to comfort their grieving father, and now eternally pursued by another man-turned-star called Orion from the other side of the night sky. I'd repeated the peculiar names after him until I knew them all by heart. I could still find them in the sky, even here in Oregon, and it made me feel like the world wasn't *quite* as big a place as it seemed, if the same stars could be seen both here and in Scotland too.

I missed Uncle Jamie.

I wondered if he'd gotten my letter yet.

Someday, airplanes would make letters get across the country and the ocean in no time at all. Colonel Lindbergh had proved it was possible, and it could only become easier from now on.

In my dreams, clouds chased away my view of the stars, and the clouds had shadows, and the shadows didn't match the shapes of the clouds casting them. I sat up wide awake in the darkened room, feeling sure it meant something.

152

I almost ran across the hall to ask George, but I knew he'd be grumpy if I woke him, and the longer I sat awake myself the less clear I was what the dream had reminded me of.

I got out of bed anyway. I hadn't undressed when I'd lain down earlier. I pocketed my little flashlight and stole downstairs. I could hear the murmur of Mr. and Mrs. Graham's voices through the kitchen, so instead of sneaking out the back door, I went out the front door, closing it silently behind me, and skirted around to the back, still holding Clotilde. Lindbergh's basket was down, and I saw the white shape of his head pop up over the top of the car door where he'd curled up on the passenger seat again. He leapt out and trotted over to me. A dim light flowed from the open window above me, between the not-quite closed drapes, and I heard my name.

I stood up and pressed my face against the side of the house so I could see through the gap in the drapes. Mrs. Graham was sitting up in bed, watching Mr. Graham stuffing tidy stacks of paper into his briefcase for the next day's work, and she said, "If *you* really think we have to worry about them getting up to mischief, I think you need your head examined."

Mr. Graham shrugged, but she got out of bed and kept talking as she crossed the room towards him. "He may be your son, but he has the romantic instincts of a squashed hedgie."

"I don't understand why she doesn't just kiss him first. It's not as if she's shy about going after anything else she wants."

"She has a sensible head on her shoulders," Mrs. Graham said. "And they are *twelve*. Why rush it?"

"Almost thirteen, and I'd already kissed a handful of girls by that age."

"He's not like you." She took the end of his tie and gave it a little tug, forcing him to step close to her, pulling him down so she could kiss him. The sight made me suck in air, made me feel tingly. I'd like to do that to George.

"He's not like you, either," Mr. Graham said, and for a moment I didn't breathe at all and got very lightheaded. I thought I was used to seeing them kiss, but this was a whole new level of kiss, and he was on the receiving end instead of the other way around, and as she stepped back, he amended, "He's not like you in *some* ways," and then I thought maybe I better not keep watching and slowly dropped to a crouch under the window. I could still hear them, though, and that was plenty.

I hadn't realized Mrs. Graham was such an enthusiastic participant in Mr. Graham's nonsense. She always acts as if he's being a nuisance, but now I think it's just her way of playing the game, and he knows that her annoyance is feigned and—

Lindbergh tensed beside me. Now they'd put the light out in their room, I couldn't see anything, but the dog let out a low growl and darted towards the car, barking, jumping up at the fence. He sounded as if he had his teeth sunk into something. The light came back on and Mr. Graham stepped onto the porch, tying the belt of his robe. "What is it, Lindbergh?" he called softly. He went to where the dog was bouncing and peered over the fence for some time, listening, until satisfied that Lindbergh was merely overreacting. He scooped up the dog and put him in the basket, using the rope to pulley him up to George's open window, where he leapt inside and things went quiet.

Mr. Graham sat on the back steps and lit a cigarette. Mrs. Graham didn't like him smoking in the house, so I supposed he was just taking advantage of already being outside. I watched the glowing end as his hand moved to and from his mouth. It seemed to take him forever, but eventually he stubbed it out, tossed it into the flowerpot put there for the purpose, and went inside.

I waited a little longer before walking over to the car and switching on my flashlight. The batteries were dying, so the light wasn't terribly bright, but it was enough to tell that there was nothing amiss in the car. At the fence, however, I stopped in my tracks at the sight of one of my confirmation cards lying in amongst the pansies and petunias. I stooped to pick it up and all my sleepiness drained out of me as I sniffed it.

That weird floral scent.

Hands trembling, I flipped it over.

I KNOW WHERE YOU LIVE AND I'M COMING
FOR YOU SOON.

I didn't hesitate. I crunched it up, stuffed it inside Clotilde, and slipped in the back door, sliding the lock into place, then padding to the front door and locking that, too.

And then I curled into bed again, hugging Clotilde, and praying with more earnestness than ever in my life before that my guardian angel wouldn't let that person hurt me.

AUGUST 10, 1927: WEDNESDAY

Mr. Graham brought me a bulging paper bag tonight when he got home from work. George, true to form, eyed it jealously from where he was nestled in amongst sofa cushions, knowing it was probably something edible.

It was something edible. Loads and loads of Hershey's kisses!

"Daisy Delight sent them for you," Mr. Graham said. "Sorry, George, you'll have to negotiate with Louise, but since last I recall you weren't much keen on kisses..."

George sank deeper into the sofa, his doorstop Russian novel obscuring his face, which I'm sure was going quite pink.

I squirreled the kisses into my room, then came back and plopped down beside George, who seemed determined to pretend his father's teasing hadn't happened. I watched as he read, turning pages, eyes flicking across each line. I peered at the text, catching the word "murderer", and I asked, "Are all these Russian books about murderers?"

He looked up, blinking and confused as an owl in daylight.

I pointed to the sentence I'd seen and read it out. "'And with fury, as it were with passion, the murderer falls on the body, and drags it and hacks at it; so he covered her face and shoulders with kisses'. Oh... I guess it's not about murderers, is it? What in the world are you reading?" I snatched the book away and scanned the previous paragraphs.

"*Crime and Punishment* is the one about the murderer," he said. "Give it back!"

"This is fascinating," I said, not giving it back. "I thought you didn't like spit-swapping."

"I don't! I'm... I'm skipping over the kissy bits." But his face was going red again.

"Hmm." I gave him a sly sideways grin. "I think I'd like to hear this part."

He took the book back and snapped it shut. "I don't think your mother would much like that."

"Would yours?"

"How would I know? She never reads this kind of stuff!"

Mr. Graham's shoulders shook in silent laughter in his chair in the corner. When he collected himself, he said, "It's a cautionary tale, Louise. I told George to read it so he doesn't end up like me, with a trail of broken hearts and suicidal damsels in his wake." He winked at me, and I gaped at him.

"Why don't you go set the table or something?" George muttered at me.

"I think *I'll* go set the table," Mr. Graham said, fleeing the room, leaving the two of us alone in awkward silence.

George broke it at last, a blend of scorn and panic in his voice. "I don't want to kiss any girls!"

"Tell that to Olivia," I shot back. "Anyway, nobody asked you to kiss them. It's just funny that you're reading about it, that's all. After all your fuss!"

"Lots of books have kissing," he reasoned aloud. "Even the Bible has kissing. It doesn't mean anything, reading about it. Or... skipping over it, like I'm doing."

"Except you're not skipping over it, are you?" I said. "It's okay to enjoy things, you know." I felt unexplainably grumpy all of a sudden. Was George secretly interested in kissing and just too proud to admit it, or was he really skipping the kissy bits because they embarrassed him?

I stalked out of the room just as George called out, "Wait, what does Olivia have to do with anything?"

I didn't turn back to answer, leaving him alone to stew over his cautionary tale full of unpronounceable names, and went to my room, where I proceeded to line up my shining foil-wrapped kisses along my windowsill. There were thirty-seven of them—a prime amount, if you ask me. Why in the world did Daisy Delight have thirty-seven kisses just sitting around the office? Did she flirt with Mr. Graham, like that advertisement where the boy waits with pursed lips while the girl holds up a Hershey's kiss, the one captioned "A Kiss for You"? It didn't seem her style, but I could see Mr. Graham doing it. He was *ridiculously* flirtatious with D. D., largely because she was old and crotchety and clearly could have used someone like him in her life a hundred years ago.

I am not quite thirteen and I already feel old and crotchety and could use someone in my life who wants to kiss me now.

I unwrapped a kiss and popped it into my mouth. The taste of the chocolate made me realize I was really, really hungry, but not for anything else in the world but more chocolate. I unwrapped three more and stuffed them all into my mouth at once, dividing the remaining ones into three families of eleven.

Nothing had ever felt (or tasted) so satisfying in my life before.

I came downstairs with one kiss family in my hand, just in time to hear the call to supper.

We'd barely sat down, and I'd just set Mr. and Mrs. Kiss and the three eldest Kiss children beside my plate when Mr. Graham started in on George about his book again, which he had brought to the table with him, and instead of feeling any sympathy for George's discomfort, I just got mad. I hurled the six remaining Kiss children down and stalked off upstairs.

Mrs. Graham, not Mother, was once again the one who came knocking on my door not long afterwards. (Why not Mother? I guess she didn't know what to do with me.) I was scowling as she let herself in and had a seat on the edge of my bed, clasping her hands around her knees. "I hope you didn't want those kisses back, because I'm afraid my son has already devoured them."

I muttered something uncharitable from deep in my rocking chair, where I was slouching in the most unladylike manner possible.

"I think," she said, contemplating some distant thing, "that he will eventually notice you. Give him time."

I glanced at her suspiciously.

"Nobody's said a word to him," she said, her mouth twitching in amusement. "I told George's father I'd divorce him if he breathed a word."

"You wouldn't!"

"Possibly not, but I know ways to make him compliant."

I thought of the aggressiveness I'd observed through the window the other night and realized there was a facet of Mrs. Graham the world at large didn't see, and decided she was probably right.

"Anyway, it is very obvious. Your feelings for George, I mean."

"Not obvious to *him*," I said.

"You have to be very specific with George. You know that."

I did know that. "I will never ask him to kiss me. If he doesn't ever think to do it on his own, I don't want it."

She fixed me with a thoughtful look. "That's your prerogative, of course, but it wouldn't be wrong for you to ask. Is there some particular reason why you don't want to?"

I bit my lip, considering. Was it just me being bullheaded and stupid? After a few moments, I said, "I guess I don't want to make anyone think they're obligated to feel a certain way. It's... well, I tell George 'go' and he goes, or 'do this' and he does it. You know? And I want him to think of it, on his own."

I looked up and there was compassion and understanding in Mrs. Graham's eyes. "There is something to be said for George," she mused, "and that is, he's guaranteed never to burst into your place inebriated in the middle of the night on a mission to ravish you. Without first finding out if you mind him doing so." Again there was some amusement in her face, as if she hadn't been particularly bothered by the incident in question then or now. She saw my face and laughed aloud. "We are anything but ideal role models, Louise. I stand by that though—if George ever comes to you and kisses you without first asking five ways if it's acceptable and you mind, I will... I will... eat a spoonful of lard!"

We both had a good laugh over that, then she stood up and smoothed her skirt. "He's left for Rabbi Zylberman's, if you want to come down and get your dinner."

"Okay," I said, and followed her down. After I ate, I decided to go weed the pansy bed, because I'd noticed even with just my pathetic flashlight the other night that it was looking a bit overgrown. As I tossed the juicy weeds to an appreciative trio of inquisitive hens, I saw a ripped piece of fabric in amongst the flowers: a small shred of sturdy cloth, the kind Daddy's work pants used to be made of. I flashed back to the other night when Lindbergh had been going nuts over my stalker, and I felt sure he'd torn off this scrap from the pants of someone escaping over the fence. I rubbed my thumb over it thoughtfully a while before pocketing it to contemplate later.

After I finished weeding, I washed my hands and returned to my room, using my street-facing window as a barre to do some dance practice as I watched the passersby below me, their evening shadows angling far into the street, rippling over the uneven bits of the road.

One shadow didn't move. One shadow belonged to someone I couldn't see, someone who thought the thick tree he stood behind obscured him from detection by me.

I KNOW WHERE YOU LIVE AND I'M COMING FOR YOU SOON.

I backed away, filled with fear.
The poison pen was watching now.
When I peeked again, his shadow was gone.

AUGUST 16, 1927: TUESDAY

*T*hings have been a little strained between George and me since *Anna Karenina* and the Hershey Kiss Explosion. (I don't like that this is becoming a more common occurrence between us.) I got another period a couple days after, and I moped in my room, most of the time. I don't think George even noticed, so engrossed in his Cautionary Tale was he. I missed him, but I was still mad at him.

And then it passed, and I wondered why in the world such a silly thing had made me so mad in the first place.

I still had twenty-two kisses on my windowsill: two families of eleven. I decided to save them for my next crisis, whenever that might come. (I'll just tell you now. It was about a month later. Who could have guessed that periods make you grumpy AND give you an insatiable need for chocolate?) I was sure I'd never waste kisses by rage-throwing them at George again, but would instead hoard them like the dragon I'd told Margie I was under the underwear. (CHOCOLATE kisses, you understand. I'd give him the other kind if he wanted.)

George was the one to make up whatever had gone wrong between us, so maybe he did actually notice. I mentioned before that gorgeous copy of *We* in the bookshop window display. Well, we were passing it this afternoon on our way to ballet class, and I paused to ogle it through the window. I longed SO much for a copy of my own, but I'd spent my last money on that plane ride, and I hated to ask Mother for something so frivolous as a book for me, The Girl Who Doesn't Read.

Anyway, George went inside and came out a few minutes later with the blue and gold volume in his hands. He pushed it at me and said, a bit gruffly, "Come on, we're going to be late."

I just stood there speechless, then had to hurry to catch up with him because he hadn't stopped walking.

"You're giving it to me?" I asked.

"Obviously."

"Gee, thanks!"

He shrugged, but there was a hint of a smirk that told me he was pleased at my being pleased. I'd bought him things occasionally, back in Turner, when I'd had money and he didn't, but it was odd to have the roles reversed.

And it was the first time he'd ever given me a present that wasn't for my birthday or Christmas, and it made me SOARINGLY happy inside.

I showed it off to Olivia and the other girls when we were changing. Olivia seemed in awe that George had given me something, and also jealous that it wasn't her who'd received it.

When we got home, I sat on the sofa and just held it in my hands, eyes riveted on the dark blue cover with the golden silhouette of the *Spirit of St. Louis* between the title and Colonel Lindbergh's name. Would I someday write a book about flying? Would I have the chance to be the first girl to do something really fantastic in aviation that everyone would want to read about?

Finally I opened it. First there was a photograph of Colonel Lindbergh and his plane, then the title page, then the long list of impressions. My copy was from the *eleventh impression* since the book was released two months ago! I don't know how many books they print with each impression, but he must be getting rich off the sales, not to mention the $25,000 in prize money from Mr. Orteig, for crossing the Atlantic first.

George came in and asked if I wanted to read it myself or have him do it. I held it out, grinning, and he sprawled out the full length of the sofa and put his feet on my lap. I pushed them off with mock disdain, although secretly I'd have liked to let him leave them there. (For the sake of clarity, he also puts his feet on his parents' laps, so there's nothing particularly special about him doing it to me. Color yourselves shocked.) Anyway, he laughed, and he said, "I suppose you want to skip the introduction and get right to the—"

"THE WHOLE THING," I protested, then realized he was just in a very impish mood. I pulled a footstool over so I could sit next to him as he lay there and be able to see the words as he read, and the pictures as they came.

But soon I closed my eyes and just let the words paint their own pictures in my mind. The glamor and romance of Colonel Lindbergh's nomadic, independent life beckoned me.

As we were getting ready for bed later, I called George to my room and whispered, "The poison pen knows where I live."

He didn't seem surprised at the idea that the sort of man who stalks children to scare them with anonymous notes would have learned where I lived. "How do you know?"

So I told him a censored version of my accidental backyard spy mission of the other night, and showed him the fabric scrap and the latest note. "And also I saw his shadow from behind the tree on the corner there, last week."

"Why are you only just now telling me about this?" he asked mildly, peering out the window.

"I don't know. I kind of... let myself forget afterwards, I guess. I'm tired of thinking about it."

"Well, you need to not be tired of thinking about it. He's obviously not going anywhere. You didn't see which way he went, I guess?"

I shook my head. "I stepped away from the window so he couldn't see me."

George checked that the windows were locked. "I don't like the idea of you sleeping here anymore," he said. "You're the only one on this side of the house. If he was to prop a ladder up here, nobody would hear or see it. So, you either need to find a reason to camp out with your mother or come use my couch."

It wasn't really a question. I was not about to give my mother a reason to become an inquisitor or worry her with the truth. So I scooped up my blankets and pillow and Clotilde and followed George into his room, making myself comfortable on his couch while he let down the basket to bring Lindbergh up for the night.

The puppy bounded over to me to say hello, but when he leapt up to my lap, he lurched backwards with a little growl.

"That's weird," George said, coming over to try calming the agitated dog. "Hey, boy, it's just Louise!"

"I don't think it's me," I said. "I think he doesn't like Clotilde."

Lindbergh lunged at Clotilde, attempting to grab her in his teeth, but I held her out of reach.

"I guess I better take her out," I said. "I wonder why he's acting like that. He wasn't bothered by her the other night when he was sitting in the roses with me before I found the card..."

I put my carrot back in my room, and Lindbergh settled back to normal. "Maybe he doesn't like orange," George said.

"Maybe."

AUGUST 17, 1927: WEDNESDAY

*I*t was such an ordinary day, to begin with.

There was a recipe for darkening greying hair in the paper. Well, not a recipe, *exactly*—it just said to use sage tea and sulphur, but it didn't give proportions. At breakfast I told Mrs. Graham she should try it, and she laughed and said she'd earned every one of her grey hairs and didn't want Mr. Graham to forget it, thank-you-very-much, which statement Mr. Graham replied to by pinching her somewhere she didn't expect. Then chasing her into the other room, where she kept trying to protest, and he kept shutting her up with kisses.

"I'd like *my* hair to be 'dark and glossy'," I said, loudly, trying to cover up their noise. "Maybe I'll try it myself."

"Be careful," George warned. "It might just turn it green and you'll have to chop it all off like Anne Shirley."

"It's already chopped," I pointed out, "and green hair might be interesting. At least it's a color!"

"Please don't," Mother said, sighing. "School starts in a month. It would be disgraceful."

I went to the mirror above one of the little half-circle table things at the edge of the dining room and inspected my reflection. My almost-white hair would probably darken to the color of wheat at best.

I caught Mother eyeing me in the reflection, her own hair so very like mine, and said to her, "Don't you ever mind it?"

She gave me a small smile. "There are women who pay a good deal of money for what we have for free."

"I suppose," I agreed reluctantly, turning away from the mirror.

Mrs. Graham was still perfectly cheerful when George and I left to walk with Mr. Graham on his way to work, as far as the park in front of the capitol building, where we waved him on his way. We stayed with Lindbergh, our pockets full of dog biscuits, teaching the puppy to sit. It involved a great deal of dog biscuit bribery and much running after him as he got distracted by squirrels.

And dust motes.

And his own shadow.

And then it was back to the house for lunch, only it was too quiet as we walked in. Usually Mother would be playing music, but today she met us as we came in and said in a low voice that Mrs. Graham wasn't well. "What happened?" George asked, hanging up Lindbergh's leash.

"Someone hacked up her rose bush in the night," Mother said. "She didn't notice until she went out to water after you left."

George and I went out to look at the bush in question. Mrs. Graham had at least ten different roses back there, but the white one under her bedroom window—the one I'd hid beside the other night— was her particular obsession for reasons George didn't understand. It had been very brutalized. I could see where she'd used splints and cord to try to encourage it to grow back together, and imagined her grim, tearful face as she'd worked. Some of it must have been too damaged to bother with, as there were several branches neatly stacked in the bed beside the bush. It gave me chills seeing it, considering that the one she loved best had been targeted over the others, and I think George was having the same thought. It was getting bigger and darker, this evil following us.

The afternoon felt somber. George made us lunch, but even he seemed distracted and didn't eat much. I'm not sure it had anything to do with the rose bush, though. It seemed to start after he asked me why I wasn't getting ready for dance, and I said, "George, it's Wednesday."

"Oh," he said, his face clouding a bit. "So it is." And he disappeared to his room.

I cleaned up the kitchen. Mother was sitting beside Mrs. Graham on her bed, holding her hand and speaking softly to her on occasion.

When Mr. Graham came home from work, I took his hat and briefcase and informed him about the rose bush. He said something under his breath that sounded like, "Not Yvonne..." as he rushed off to see for himself and commiserate with his wife.

Mother emerged and George appeared at the foot of the stairs with his bookladen knapsack. "Who's Yvonne?" I asked, perplexed.

"It's the rose," he said. "Yvonne Rabier."

"I don't think he meant the rose," I said, although I couldn't explain why I felt so sure. George just shrugged and left with an absent-minded wave to go study with Rabbi Zylberman.

I know he was only gone for half an hour, because Mother insists I practice at *least* that long each day, and my eye was on the clock the whole time, because I wasn't in the mood to practice. The house seemed permeated with a darkness I could feel, and I kept my playing as quiet as possible.

When George came back in, he didn't stop or speak, just ran straight up the stairs before I could say a word. I ran after him, but he slammed his door shut before I made it to him and I heard the key turn in the lock.

"George!" I called. He didn't answer, and I couldn't see through the keyhole since the key was in the way. But, since usually he's so absorbed in those sessions with Rabbi Zylberman that two or three hours often went by before he came home, I knew something had gone terribly wrong tonight.

I waited a few minutes before shauchling back down. Mrs. Graham had emerged, her eyes red-rimmed in her pale face, and had her hand on the rail to go upstairs when the telephone jingled. She went to answer it, and as she reached to pick it up I stage whispered, "Something's not right with George! He's home already."

She glanced at me as if she wasn't sure I'd spoken, and scarcely had time to say "Hello?" before I could hear Rabbi Zylberman's voice shouting down the line. Mrs. Graham, knuckles white as she gripped the receiver, held it away from her ear, and I leaned in so I could hear better. I don't think she even noticed me.

"That boy of yours, whom I have spent so much valuable time instructing, just told me he's decided he can be a Christian Jew and wants to be baptized instead of having a bar mitzvah ceremony!"

Mrs. Graham winced, letting herself slide down against the wall to a crouch on the floor. Her voice, drained from a day of tears, was flat. "It's the first I've heard of this, Rabbi."

"Perhaps you can talk some sense into him, young lady," he went on, relentless. "He wouldn't listen to reason. He had the insolence to walk out without answering me!"

Personally, knowing the rabbi, I suspected his idea of "reasoning with George" was more akin to "ranting at George". Mrs. Graham blinked back fresh tears as she said, "Rabbi, I told George I would allow him to choose his own path. He needed time to learn and think things through, and I know he deeply appreciates everything you've taught him—"

"Only a few months until he's thirteen, too!"

"Would you rather have bar mitzvahed him and then have him tell you he planned to be baptized?" Her grip on the receiver tightened even more.

At that point the rabbi switched to Yiddish, perhaps to keep the nosy telephone operator in the dark, and for five solid minutes they fought one another before Mrs. Graham snapped. "Talk to me about it Friday night after you've had time to cool down."

"ME cool down!" he said, to which she shouted one last thing that was a lot of Yiddish peppered with occasional *Yvonnes* before slamming down the phone and setting off upstairs with me at her heels.

She rapped sharply on the door. "George?" she demanded.

"Go away," he said, in a not-fierce voice that sounded suspiciously like crying.

She waited a moment before adding, in that odd flat tone, "I did say I'd leave the choice to you, and it's not as though I'm a good Jew myself..." before shutting herself into the bathroom, where I heard her crying in a way that terrified me. The phone jingled again downstairs, and this time Mr. Graham answered it and told Rabbi Z something to the effect of "this is not the time, you have no idea what you're doing to her" before he too slammed down the receiver and came upstairs. When he realized the bathroom door was locked, a look of panic crossed his face, and he fished a key from his waistcoat pocket to let himself in. The crying continued as he held her, trying to soothe her, but she was incoherent and hysterical. Mother appeared after a few minutes with a glass of water and something clenched in her fist. I don't think they even noticed me from where I crouched in my shadowy corner. They were too busy trying to calm Mrs. Graham, who was fighting and kicking at her husband. He pinned her wrists behind her back after she tried to hit him, and Mother got her to swallow whatever that pill was in her hand, and after a minute Mrs. Graham seemed to lose whatever fight she'd had, and he let go of her wrists, pulling her drooping body into his arms and kissing the top of her head.

"I should be dead," she whispered.

"No," he said, gentle but firm. "None of that, hen. Let's get you into bed, shall we?"

With Mother and Mr. Graham on either side of her, Mrs. Graham made her way down. I followed and slipped onto the back porch without them noticing. A few minutes later, Mr. Graham came out and sank heavily onto the steps beside me, fishing out his cigarettes and attempting to light up, but his hand shook too much, so I held it still for him. "Thanks," he whispered, and took a deep drag, exhaling a cloud.

"What happened?" he asked me, his voice as devoid of emotion as his wife's had been earlier. "Not the rose. Just now. What was the rabbi on about?"

"George told Rabbi Zylberman he wanted to be baptized, and the rabbi and Mrs. Graham argued over the phone about it."

"Oh, God." He leaned his face into one hand. It didn't sound like swearing, more like a prayer.

"Why does the rose bush matter?" I asked after a moment.

He'd already sucked the first cigarette to nothing and lit a second before he answered. "It's her story to tell, not mine, but it—let's just say she associates that particular rose with something precious and painful. She didn't need any drama with George on top of it. She blames herself too much for things outside her control." He sighed out smoke again and looked up at the sky. "She defied tradition naming

George after me, did you know that? They don't believe in naming children after living relatives. She did it anyway. out of spite. She's said before all the trouble we've had is her being punished for that." He laughed humorlessly. "I sometimes think she regrets that more than, you know, that little detail of the adulterous alliance with me."

Lindbergh came up and Mr. Graham absentmindedly scratched him behind his ears. His eyes wandered to the mutilated rose bush, and he made a sound alarmingly like he was trying not to cry, and whispered again, "Yvonne."

None of us thought of supper. Whatever Mother had given Mrs. Graham had put her to sleep, and when I left Mr. Graham on the steps with his third cigarette, Mother was sitting in the chair beside Mrs. Graham's bed, hands clasped and still. I sat on the couch in the front room until Mother went up to bed, and I followed a few minutes later.

I could see the lamp was still on in George's room, the light spilling in a narrow strip from under his door, but it was still locked and I wasn't about to sleep in my room, so I wrapped myself in the blanket I kept folded at the foot of my bed and, hugging Clotilde, parked myself in front of George's door, so it would be impossible for him to exit without my knowledge.

172

August 18, 1927: Thursday

*I*t's not very comfortable sleeping (or in my case not sleeping) sitting up on a hard wooden floor. George's light had never gone off, and when his alarm clock rang, I put Clotilde and my blanket away and made my silent trek downstairs.

One dim lamp still burned by the Grahams' bed, and I could see Mr. Graham had fallen asleep propped up on his pillows with Mrs. Graham in his arms. I stepped into the back yard where the bicycles were. It wasn't long before George appeared, newsbag over his shoulder and dog under his arm.

He leapt back in shock when I emerged from the shadows. "Gosh sakes, Louise!" he hissed in annoyance, dumping Lindbergh into the wire basket on his bike.

"I'm coming with you," I said.

"I don't want to talk," he said grumpily.

"I'm not asking you to talk," I said. "But I don't want you to be alone, either." He shrugged and mounted his bike, tearing down the street with me in hot pursuit.

The city had a weird, hollow feeling at that hour of the morning. It thunked me right back in time to when we ran away two years ago and were wandering the streets of Portland well after midnight.

Unsettling, certainly.

I helped George fold his papers. He alone of all the boys was completely silent, and my presence seemed to hold them back from ribbing him about it. As we rode through the crisp pre-dawn air, I wished I could make him feel better.

After he'd made all his deliveries and we'd deposited the bicycles back at home, George stuffed his hands into his pockets and said, "I'm not ready to go in."

I wasn't either. The heavy, mysterious grief blanketing Mrs. Graham had shaken me more than I cared to admit. Out here felt better. "Well, let's walk then," I said. I took Lindbergh's leash in my hand and kept pace with George as he strode off down the sidewalk.

We wandered for a very long time, not really going any place particular, just walking through endless silent neighborhoods. Finally, without preamble, George said, "He told me my choice was a betrayal."

I knew he meant Rabbi Zylberman. "Are you having second thoughts, then?"

"No." He stopped and slumped his back against the nearest telephone pole and stared at the ground for several minutes. "I'm not having second thoughts. He brought up the topic of a bar mitzvah ceremony a couple weeks ago, and I realized I didn't want it."

"What is it?" I asked.

"It means son of the commandment. That when I'm thirteen I'm responsible for myself, and that I would be obligated to help lead in prayers and readings at Sabbath services. The thing is, just being thirteen is enough. There's no law that you *have* to have a ceremony. I still become bar mitzvah in December with or without a ceremony. He knows that. So does Mamma." He took a deep breath. "I decided… I decided I could be both Jewish and follow Jesus, too. I hadn't thought it possible a few months ago, and it was torture. I thought there was a hard, uncrossable line and I'd have to pick a side, until Dr. Beskin came."

After another long pause, he began walking again. "I've written

174

him twice with loads of questions, and he's been so kind and answered them all and then some. He helped clear my head. Mamma and Rabbi Zylberman both think Messiah is yet to come, and that Jesus and Christianity are completely irrelevant outside of the fact that Christians have consistently treated us like trash over the centuries. Uncle Jamie doesn't think Judaism is relevant anymore because Christianity superseded it—which makes me feel twitchy. I tried explaining to him why that made me feel uncomfortable, but I'm not sure if he understood." He huffed. "Anyway, it feels like magnets pushing each other the wrong way around. But Dr. Beskin says one is a continuation of the other, not a replacement. Christianity doesn't cancel out Judaism. He says if people truly followed the teachings of Jesus, there wouldn't be racism or antisemitism in the Christian world, and social justice would just *be*. That if Christians realized how much they're missing by not reverencing the Old Testament the same way they do the New Testament, they'd see Jesus is all through the Bible, really, if you look. In Torah too."

George was in full preacher mode now, his hands expressive as he went on and on for a very long time as we continued our meander through the streets until we found a curb to sit on (except for Lindbergh, who bounced), and all the time George kept talking. It was as if he'd been holding it all in for such a long time and it simply wouldn't stay in a minute longer. I didn't understand everything, but I got the general idea.

"So I don't really agree with everything the Presbyterian church believes," he was saying, "but I don't think I have to. I can still be baptized there. And someday when I'm a minister I'm going to try hard to help people see the thread that runs from Genesis straight through to Revelation. But I have to study a lot first, to make it clear in my own head."

"You have a few years," I commented drily, wondering why he was so darned eager to be an adult already.

And then there was a long, long silence, as if someone had shut off the verbal tap. George yawned noisily and flopped back on the grass. "I didn't sleep much last night. I'm knackered."

"*I* didn't sleep at all," I said.

"And I'm starving."

"When are you *not*?"

He hauled himself up with a sheepish grin. "I guess we should be getting back. I hope Mamma's okay."

"They gave her something to help her sleep," I said, and we trudged homewards. The sky was no longer black.

We were a couple blocks from home when Lindbergh pulled at his leash, refusing to budge, and growling. It was just like when he'd refused to be in the same room as Clotilde. George and I looked at each other, then around us. My skin prickled.

Lindbergh's growling was focused on a large potted plant sitting at the end of someone's sidewalk. Its scent wafted up to me, strong and familiar and disturbing.

"It's the flower the note papers all smell like," I whispered. "Like they'd been drowned in some granny's perfume."

"It's a gardenia," George said, as if it was obvious. (How does he *know* these things?)

I took his hand and pulled him along with me, willing myself not to run. George scooped up Lindbergh, since he wouldn't walk. A moment later, something hit the back of my head, and I turned. Lindbergh wriggled out of George's arms and pawed at a bit of card folded into a dart that had fallen at our feet. George bent to retrieve it, unfolded it, angling it so the streetlight lit the text, then looked up at me. "It's one of your confirmation cards," he said. "Like the last one." He flipped it over, and even in the uncertain light I saw the color drain from his face. "I think it's time to tell Dad," he whispered, hoarsely, and his hand trembled as he passed it my way.

GUESS WHO WON'T BE COMING HOME ALIVE
TONIGHT.

There was no drawing, no hints as to which of us was meant by this threat, but George was right. Supposing it was Mr. Graham at risk? We would all be sunk, with nobody to look after us, if something happened to him.

"He's here," I whispered. "I feel it."

As if to confirm my words, Lindbergh growled and crouched as if preparing to pounce on something behind us.

Everything happened so fast after that. George scooped up Lindbergh again and called out to me to hurry up and run. I stuffed the note into my pocket and tried to follow, but panic had frozen my legs.

Halfway across the street ahead of me, Lindbergh leapt out of George's arms for the third time and came growling and snapping at a run back towards me. Instead of coming after him, George pitched sideways as if he'd just been hit by something, just as a car screeched to a halt where he was. That unfroze me, but I'd barely lifted one foot before a big hand clapped itself over my mouth and turned me away from the scene, so I couldn't see whether George had been killed.

I kicked and flailed, but there is only so much you can do when your assailant has the advantage of surprise, and you can't see who's got you but his grip indicates he's three times as large as you, and your best friend might have just left you preemptively widowed.

And also—also I thought of Sam. Honestly, all thoughts of George left my mind the second that hand grabbed me. I only thought, *Sam is back against all odds and going to make good on his hideous unspeakable threat.* Those hands held on to me relentlessly, pushing me forward. I could hear Lindbergh still barking, somewhere not far off. There must have been a second man, too, because someone tied my hands behind my back and dropped a bag over my head. I was shoved into a car and heard a click I assumed was a cocking pistol, and a hoarse man's voice breathed near my ear. "One peep and you're dead, got that?"

I nodded my head inside the bag—itchy, hot thing!

(I'd choose death over what Sam threatened, though, and resolved in that instant I *would* scream if I had to, just to make it stop.)

Anyway, there was a lurch as the car drove off. It wasn't a long drive, but it was very disorienting. My fear kept me from being able to keep accurate track of how many turns we took and in which directions. At last we stopped, and I was carried like a sack of potatoes to a room where they took the bag off my head. My eyes strained to see my captors, but the sun had not yet properly risen and I could barely make out their shapes, let alone their faces. Before I could think to scream, one of them deftly gagged me.

He was not as deft about tying me and my feet to the chair I'd been pushed into, however, because after they'd left me alone and the weak daylight came shyly through the transom window, I was able to see it was a haphazard tangle of knots in an inordinate quantity of rope.

The room stayed very dim, and boring silence surrounded me. I couldn't make noise myself, no thanks to the (clean, I hoped) cotton rags stuffed into my mouth. I threw my weight around as much as possible, but only managed to tip my chair over backwards. And then, because that was ridiculous, I eventually got it to roll sideways. It wasn't any more comfortable, but it left me with a trace of dignity and took the weight off my hands.

The silence was spooky. Whoever had brought me here must surely be nearby guarding me, but I could hear absolutely nothing, not even automobiles passing outside. So I did some mental arithmetic and relived my Waco flight to distract myself.

My eyes began to grow heavy, and I thought of Colonel Lindbergh, awake in the air for thirty-three and a half hours. His life and success had depended on that. Mine might too. I'd already been awake for more than twenty-four hours, since the sun had appeared to be fully up a while ago, and I had never been so tired in my life.

I tried very hard to stay awake, I really did. But it was no use. I still passed out cold in the end.

I don't know how long I was asleep, but when I woke again, the daylight was the more golden color that comes after noon, and it was brighter, which made me think the source of the light must be facing the west. My brain and body having received the rest they needed, I instantly became furious at the stupidity of my just lying here not even trying to get free. I hadn't survived all Sam's threats and cruelty just to give up and quit now.

Stay angry, little one, you're going to need it.

The side of my face had gone numb from being pressed so long against the gritty, cold floor, and I started looking around the room as best I could from my awkward vantage point.

The first thing, of course, was to find a way to untie myself. The

rope truly was tangled, but my squirming about earlier seemed to have loosened the ones around my arms. Maybe my captors had tried to compensate for lousy knots by winding more rope?

It took ages, but eventually I did work my hands out, although it left my wrists and palms raw and burning. I got the rags out of my mouth next, then undid my ankles and removed my shoes so nobody would hear my footsteps.

The only light in the room came from that transom window above a door with a textured glass pane in it, and it wasn't a lot of light. I pressed my ear to the door and listened.

Silence still, dead silence. What *was* this place? The doorknob didn't turn. There must be a way to lock it from outside.

I picked up the chair, but it slipped out of my stiff hands and made a loud clatter as I tried to place it against the door. I froze, but only silence continued all around me. I climbed onto the seat, but

I wasn't tall enough to see out, so I stepped onto the doorknob and prayed I wouldn't slip off as I peered through the transom.

This room was one of several along a corridor. A line of offices? No other people in sight, and the source of light was a big window at the end of the hall. The other end had a stairwell.

I climbed down and sat in the chair, considering my options. If only George were here, so we could put our brains to combined use!

And then it finally sunk in that he'd been thrown down in the street and hit by a car. I felt a deeper panic then, wondering if he'd survived it, and what I would do if he hadn't.

GUESS WHO WON'T BE COMING HOME ALIVE TONIGHT.

I covered my mouth with my hands. Maybe he'd been the intended target, and a third accomplice had driven the car that hit him. The idea of a Georgeless future was so bleak I couldn't bear it.

And if *I* couldn't bear it, what about Mrs. Graham, already deep into one of her pits of despair? It would kill her.

I don't know how long I sat there suffering from delayed shock, but eventually I managed to get hold of myself. George or no George, Mother would be frantic with worry over *me*.

I stood on the chair to study the transom window again. I was pretty sure I could squish through it, and I did have plenty of rope, but without someone there to hoist me up so I could go feet first...

I huffed impatiently. I'd likely have to break the textured glass in the door itself if I was ever going to get out.

I sat on the floor and emptied the contents of my pockets into my lap. They weren't very promising: paper clips and strings, a pencil, this morning's poison pen note, my knife, and one of my peppermint stick bits. I brushed lint and dog biscuit crumbs off the candy and began to "smoke" it, huffing again, slouching as I sucked at it. *Engage, brain. Come up with something.*

GUESS WHO WON'T BE COMING HOME ALIVE TONIGHT.

Maybe the car that hit George had nothing to do with my captors' evil plan at all. What *was* their plan? Certainly extorting ransom money was out of the question. They would more likely just kill me. Maybe they were waiting until it was dark to come back and see to the murder part.

If that was true, I probably didn't have a terribly long time left to live. It didn't hurt to be prepared for that extremity. On the front of the defaced confirmation card, around the edges of the design, I wrote:

Last W & T of LBP. G can have all my stuff. I love you, Mother. I'm sorry you didn't kiss me, G.

Then I scratched out the last line and stuffed everything back into my pockets except the knife. I considered throwing it blade-first at the textured glass pane, but it would make noise, and I couldn't risk that. Just because the building was quiet and nobody was visible in the hall didn't mean I wasn't being guarded. It would have to be the transom window or nothing.

I made a sort of ladder from the rope—a series of loop footholds—taking pride in the fact that I, a *girl* of twelve, made better knots than my presumably male adult captors had managed. (Thank you, Daddy, for one more proof that you were a good man, teaching me useful life skills.)

I tied my shoelace ends together so I could hang my shoes around my neck, buttoning them inside my cardigan to stop them swinging about.

Then, perched precariously on the doorknob again, I fastened the top of the rope around the rod that opened the transom.

"Here goes nothing," I muttered grimly to myself, and with the aid of the rope and my ballet-induced flexibility, I hauled myself up and squeezed through, thankful for the first and only time in my life that I had the figure of a toothpick, and dropped lightly to the floor on the other side.

The key that had kept me imprisoned still stuck out of the doorknob. I pocketed it as a souvenir and tiptoed down the corridor to the window at the end, only to see that the building across the alley blocked any definite view of the sun's position. Oh, what I wouldn't have given for Uncle Jamie's pocket watch with its compass fob right then! And I was three floors up.

When would they be coming back for me?

I tried each door along the hall, and they all swung open to vacant, eerie rooms whose floors were littered with peeling paint curls and dust.

I crept down the stairwell and found the same was true for the next floor.

The ground floor windows must have been boarded up, because that level was pitch black. They'd brought me to an *abandoned* building?! Had they locked me in here to starve to death, then?

I went back up the stairs so I had light to put my shoes back on. Who knew what sorts of sharp debris might be on the floor in that darkness?

I wasn't scared of the dark itself, but in a place like this, I was uneasy just not knowing what might jump out at me from that darkness.

They got me in here, I thought. *There must be a cleverly disguised entrance somewhere.*

It took ages for me to shuffle my way to the nearest hairline crack of light between window boards. I felt all around, but of course the boards had been nailed on from outside. I thought perhaps I could push hard enough to break them free, but no such luck. I only got a sore shoulder for my trouble. No amount of strength would make them budge.

My eyes had adjusted by this time as much as it was possible for them to do. The light filtering dimly down the stairwell showed me that this room, unlike the ones above, was open, with pillars for supports and heaps of indeterminate objects about. It was hopelessly huge. There was no efficient way to search for the entrance without a flashlight, and a little wandering soon showed me that the heaps of objects were arranged in an almost maze-like fashion. It would take too long and I didn't have that kind of time.

So I went back upstairs, to the big window at the end of the corridor, and looked down. Even from the second floor, it was a substantial drop. I estimated it was eighteen feet, at least.

Since it had become obvious nobody was inside, and the waning light was becoming alarming, I didn't worry about making noise as I clattered back up to the room where I'd been imprisoned to fetch the rope and return to the lower window. I stood back several feet and aimed my opened knife at the center of the glass. It shattered with satisfying thoroughness, and I stood listening for several seconds to see if the noise roused any alarm.

It didn't. I could hear the distant sounds of traffic now, though.

I leaned out, careful to avoid the ragged glass around the edge, and dangled my rope of footholds. It only reached part of the way down, leaving enough distance I'd have to jump that it gave me pause. I didn't need to break any bones just as I was effecting an escape at last. I pulled the rope back in, biting my lip, making decisions.

I stripped off my clothes so I could shed the long underwear, then put my dress back on and, with help from my teeth, tore the underwear into strips to lengthen the rope. With my stockings added at the end, I was confident it would get me close enough to the ground to be safe.

I felt prickly-cold and naked without my woolen armor, but it was about to save my life. Just not in the way I'd once envisioned.

I secured the top end of the rope to the radiator pipe under the window and gingerly picked my way over the glass bits on the sill, then slowly began my descent.

At the end of the stockings, I let go, dropping into a heap of old leaves and rubbish. It was growing dusky in the alley, and I was increasingly worried about being lost in the dark in an unfamiliar area of Salem, but I paused long enough to locate my knife before moving toward the street.

Peeking around the corner, I could see I was in a maze of warehouses that seemed barren of activity. However, I could now pinpoint the sun's position as low in the west, so I strode eastward as fast as I could, open knife in hand. It wasn't much of a weapon, but it was all I had.

Gradually I came to a more inhabited area with cars going by. I spied a drug store, the owner of which was locking up. I rushed to him, waving my arms and shouting, and he turned, alarmed at the sight of me. (I did not realize until later that I was covered in grey dust and cobwebs and looked as if I'd stepped out of Miss Havisham's closet. Plus, you know, the knife.) I begged him, "Please! I have to use your telephone! It's an emergency!"

The druggist looked at me askance. "What happened to your arms?" he asked.

I glanced down and saw my forearms had some rather nasty cuts. I hadn't felt them at all; that's a glass cut for you. "I'll explain, sir, but I have to call for help right away!"

He unlocked the door, let me in, and I asked him to lock it behind him as I picked up and asked for the Grahams' house. Nobody answered. I supposed they were all out looking for me—assuming, that is, that George hadn't been killed, in which case they'd all be prostrate with grief at the morgue.

Next I tried Mr. Graham's office, but again no answer.

So I asked for the police. The druggist, his arms folded, kept his eyes fixed on me, clearly concerned that he had a maniac on his hands.

"Young lady!" the desk sergeant exclaimed, once I'd been connected and identified myself. "We've got people out everywhere looking for you! Are you all right? Where are you?"

"Where am I?" I asked the druggist. He told me the address. The policeman said someone would come collect me presently.

The clock above the druggist's counter said it was 6:17, and I slouched onto the floor in front of the counter, suddenly too knackered to stand anymore. I looked up at the druggist and explained, sleepily, "I've just escaped through a window after being kidnapped and locked up. The police are coming."

He bent down and gently extracted the knife I was still gripping, closed the blade, and laid it on the floor beside me. Then he fetched some iodine to clean my cuts with. It stung, but my exhaustion was stronger than the pain, and I fell asleep.

Until a familiar growly bark jerked me upright. "Lindbergh!" I exclaimed, and leaned forward to be slurped on by the extremely excited puppy.

Disoriented from sleep, sudden noise, and puppy slobber, it took me a moment to notice Mr. Graham and two policemen had come in. Mr. Graham pulled me to my feet and held me tightly for a long time. When he let go at last and I got a glimpse of his face, I saw how his usually pristine, collected self had completely altered. He looked

184

older, untidy, and so very exhausted. I think he'd forgotten to shave that morning, too. An unheard-of display of self-neglect!

"Where's George?" I demanded, needing to know the worst immediately.

"In hospital. We don't know much yet, just that someone found him unconscious in the street and took him in, and he only just woke up an hour ago to identify himself. Alice and your mum are with him."

"Is he hurt badly, then?" My skin crawled with dread.

"He'll live." But I saw his lips quiver the tiniest bit, and knew how utterly devastated he'd be if his boy died. But he tried to pull himself together enough to reassure me. "Dinnae fash, lass. Let's get you home so you can tell these officers what happened. We need to find out who did this."

Seated at the dining table back at the house, each of us with our own mug of hot tea, the older policeman, Officer Ferguson, asked Mr. Graham to start us off, while the younger one took out his notebook and pencil to take down his statement.

"Lindbergh—that's this boy—" Mr. Graham indicated the puppy asleep on his knees— "woke my wife and me this morning. We'd overslept. I think it was about seven-thirty. He's never done that before. The barking was so insistent, I opened the back door to see what the matter was, but he rushed inside and up the stairs. He had his lead on, which I didn't think about just then—I was still half asleep. My son George takes him along when he delivers papers, so I guess I thought it was still on from that. Upstairs, he ran into George's room, sniffing around and still barking. George wasn't there. I thought perhaps Lindbergh got away from him on his way home from delivering papers and that George would be home soon. But then the dog started scratching and howling at Louise's door. The noise woke up Louise's mother, who sleeps down the hall from both the children, and she came out to see what was going on. It didn't appear that Louise's bed had been slept in, and the dog ran straight for her doll and attacked it. Brought it over to me, growling. I got it away from him before he could destroy it, and Mrs. Pearson and I looked all over the house, in the attic and on the roof too, but neither of the children were anywhere, and it was getting on to breakfast time, so I knew something was definitely amiss. Young George never willingly skips an opportunity to eat."

We all laughed in spite of everything. He went on. "My wife, Alice, had gotten up by this time as well, so the three of us had a brief consultation, and Alice asked if we'd looked inside Louise's doll. She has buttons down her back, you see, so I went up and fetched it. Lindbergh went berserk and I had to shut him outside while we undid the buttons to feel around inside. That's where the notes were that I brought you before."

Officer Ferguson took an envelope from his pocket and shook out the all-too-familiar pieces of paper onto the table, pushing them towards me. "What can you tell us about these?" he asked me.

"You've got them out of order," I said, and rearranged them, spouting off the dates each one had shown up and the circumstances. "Wait, what's this one?"

It was a picture postcard of Inverness Castle. I flipped it over and immediately recognized Uncle Jamie's handwriting.

> *My dear girl, you NEED to tell your mother and my brother about those notes without any further delay. Please send a telegram when you receive this to let me know you've told the adults and that you are all right, because we are very concerned. I don't know that there's anything I can usefully do, but I will come if there is. Uncle Jamie*

"When did this arrive?" I asked, confused.

"Came this morning," Mr. Graham said. "Right about the time Alice had the idea of looking inside the doll. So that's when we came to report the children missing."

There was a pause as the younger officer scratched furiously to catch up, then Officer Ferguson said, "So the first two notes arrived at your dance lessons. We'll need to follow up on that. Lloyd, make a note to get a complete list of employees from the owner of the Crystal Gardens. If there's nothing else to tell me about the notes, Louise, I'd like to hear what happened this morning."

I turned to Mr. Graham and demanded, "*Did* you telegram Uncle Jamie?"

"I did," he said. "Why didn't you ever tell us about the notes?"

It was the closest to mad I think I'd ever seen him.

"This wasn't about anyone else but me," I objected. "If I told, someone would get hurt."

"You didn't tell and someone got hurt anyway," he pointed out.

I fished out the last one from my pocket and threw it down in front of him.

"That's the one from this morning." I slouched backwards into the chair, and Lindbergh deserted Mr. Graham's lap to jump onto mine.

He looked at the note, spat out one of those words we're not supposed to repeat, and flicked it towards the officers. He stood up and paced, mussing his hair even more, and at last he stopped in front of me to say, "I realize panic fogged your common sense, but—" He let out a long breath.

I said, "We were afraid that, if something happened to you, we'd all be in ten times as much danger."

"That may be true," he said. "But you're the one in that pathetic

family of yours who knows things and isn't afraid to say you know them. It's clear to me that this is the doing of one of your relatives. It's you they're after, so in that sense you're right it's not about anyone else. But to get to you, they'll frighten or harm people you love."

"You could have told us what *you* knew," I retorted. "What Mother was running from when we left Turner. I even asked you straight out. This is all related, isn't it?"

He closed his eyes, exhaling again. "She didn't want to frighten you."

I was going to make a few more accusatory comments, but Officer Ferguson lifted his hands to get our attention. "Could we please return to the topic at hand, Louise? I need to know what exactly happened this morning."

So I told him. The telephone rang as I related the details of my captivity and escape, and Mr. Graham went to answer it. By the time he returned, the policemen had stood up to go investigate my prison warehouse and see what they could learn there. We let them out, and Mr. Graham said, "That was the hospital saying George can come home. Want to come with me to collect him?"

Of course I did. I clipped on Lindbergh's leash, and we walked toward the car.

"So why did we leave Turner, then?" I asked, as I climbed into the passenger seat.

Mr. Graham rubbed the back of his head and sighed. "Somebody telephoned that morning. A caller whose voice she didn't recognize, warning her that she needed to get out of the house immediately because someone was after you."

I let out a *HA*. "Whoever it was was too late. My room had already been vandalized."

He looked up at the sky. "Why did you never say anything at the time?"

"Nobody asked."

"Louise, Louise," he said, as he started the car and settled in. He met my eyes and I met his, coolly. He looked away first.

"What else have you not told anyone?" he asked as he reversed the car into the street.

I folded my arms and cocked my head. "George skidded when he fell this morning. It looked just like how Daddy did right before he fell on his scythe."

"Did you tell the policemen that?"

"No. I only just now thought of it. At the time I didn't."

He waited for me to continue.

"Sam had a slingshot in his back pocket when he sauntered over to me after Daddy was dead. I think he shot a stone at his ankles to trip him. I think maybe someone shot at George's ankles, too. So he couldn't get out of the path of that car fast enough."

Mr. Graham stopped to let an old lady cross the street, his face deeply thoughtful. "Strengthens the theory that it's a relative. Someone extremely close to your stepfather who would imitate his methods. Any ideas?"

I shrugged, petting loose fur off Lindbergh onto the floor.

At the hospital, Mrs. Graham and Mother and George were all waiting for us in hard chairs in the lobby. Mother took me in her arms and wouldn't let go, sobbing softly into my hair. A nurse came to tell Mr. Graham exactly what had happened.

A man driving along found George unconscious in the middle of the road. His wife, who'd been a nurse before she married, was with him and said they needed to phone for an ambulance, because his right arm was broken in several places and she didn't know if other bones might also be broken. His glasses were thrown off to the side, smashed, and one side of his face was badly scraped from the pavement. So the ambulance took him in and they had to do surgery on his arm because it was such a mess. "He's lucky to be alive," the nurse said. "And lucky that the arm was all that got broken. He's also got concussion and needs to just hold still as much as possible for several days." She nattered on and on.

I glanced at Mrs. Graham, who was unkempt and dazed-looking. George looked as white as the sling his arm was in, and rather a lot as if he'd been in a brawl with a bear and lost. Mr. Graham carried him out to the car and put him in the front seat where I'd been because it was easiest, and he kind of just drooped into it and closed his eyes. He didn't even seem to notice Lindbergh climbing onto his lap.

At first George lay on his parents' bed downstairs, until the family doctor came in a few hours later to have a look at him and give him something to help him sleep. He also had a look at Mrs. Graham. I went upstairs to have a bath while he was there, to get rid of the filth of that building. It felt lovely to be clean again. I put on my nightie and Daddy's sweater and returned downstairs just as Mr. Graham was scooping up his unconscious son to carry him to his own bed.

"I'll come back in a few minutes so you can go to bed, Lydia."

"Someone needs to stay with George," Mother said. "I am happy to stay here with Alice."

"I'm *fine*," Mrs. Graham snapped. "I don't need babying."

Mr. Graham fixed her with a Look she refused to meet, and said wearily, "Listen, Alice, I'd just like to be sure you're still here in the morning, okay? We nearly lost George. I do not need the added strain of worrying over you, too. Just let Lydia stay with you, for my peace of mind."

"Everything will be fine," Mother said briskly. She shooed him out, closing the door. I trailed up after Mr. Graham, and Lindbergh followed me, his nails clicking on the floor. I turned down the blankets so George could be tucked in. Lindbergh jumped onto the bed and snuggled up to his master, unusually quiet. Mr. Graham pulled George's desk chair close to the bed and sat.

For a long time, he just watched his son, a world of love in his eyes, and he mused, "How did I end up with a boy like this? Jamie's Vincent I'd have deserved, but..." He trailed off.

"It's nothing to do with deserving," I heard myself saying. He raised his eyes to mine, but he didn't ask me to elaborate, which was good because I wasn't sure I could have explained what I meant.

I hugged myself, looking at George, so deathly white and still, and I did something I rarely, *rarely* do.

I burst into tears.

Mr. Graham looked up, startled, and held out his hand to me. I went to him and sat on his lap, feeling incredibly long and dangly, but he held me firmly as I proceeded to make his shoulder a good bit damper than it had been. He, like Lindbergh, was being unusually quiet and still, but I didn't think about that until later, because my own misery

completely blocked out everything else.

I couldn't bear it if I lost my best friend.

Mr. Graham didn't tell me to shush or stop being a baby. His fingers combed through my disastrous hair, gently teasing out the tangles, and when I'd finally cried myself out, he said, "I know I'm not your dad... or Jamie..." His voice had taken on the extra burr it always does when he's distressed or exhausted. He was certainly both just then. "But if you ever want to talk to me, about anything—I hope you know I'm here to listen and help however I can. I'm not very experienced with girls over ten," he admitted, "last having had Susan at that age before being forbidden to see her again. But I can try. I'm very fond of you, in spite of everything. I hope you know that."

There was a long silence on my part. "I guess... I guess I'm just not used to telling people my troubles," I said. "It's almost always been safer to keep my mouth shut."

"Fair enough. I know it's not easy, trusting people, after all you and your mum have been through."

"Thanks," I whispered, then turned to look at George. My hair

191

caught on Mr. Graham's unshaven face, and for some reason it made us both laugh.

"Goodness, I'm a slob," he said, shaking his head and brushing my hair free of his face.

"You had other things on your mind this morning," I reminded him. "Is George going to be okay?"

"The doctor gave him something for the pain and to help him sleep. As long as his arm stays uninfected, he'll be fine."

If it got infected, I thought, they'd have to cut it off, like Uncle Jamie had to have his foot chopped off in the war. And then my dreams of advancing to a level of dancing prowess where George could lift me off my feet and make me fly would be dashed. As soon as I had the thought I wanted to kick myself for being so shallow, and I wailed, "I don't want him to die! Not without knowing I'm so sorry!"

"Sorry for what?" Mr. Graham asked, bemused.

"Teasing him! Throwing things at him! Being... grumpy!"

Some of the tiredness in Mr. Graham's face smoothed away at that, and he smiled. "I dare say he's not too bothered by the grumpiness, if he's noticed it, which is doubtful, and having chocolate thrown at him isn't exactly something he'd complain about, either. Girls are allowed to be grumpy sometimes. At least, they *should* be allowed. It should be a law. 'Girls under the influence of emotions beyond their control not to be censured for occasional grumpiness. Free chocolate instead.' What do you think?"

I felt my face flaming. Of course Mr. Graham understood girl problems; he'd been married twice, with too many other women in his life not to know—but it was weird all the same to realize how well he understood the source of my grumps.

"Free chocolate would be fabulous," I agreed. I got to my feet and went to my windowsill, where I retrieved my last family of kisses, and piled all eleven onto George's nightstand.

Then I stood and looked at my friend and brushed his hair off his forehead, something he'd have groused about my doing if he'd been awake.

"You could kiss him," Mr. Graham said, with a wink. "He'll never know the difference."

I shook my head. It seemed wrong to kiss someone who was critically injured just because they wouldn't remember it later. I wouldn't have wanted someone to do that to me. "He feels hot," I said, worried.

"We'll give it a bit," Mr. Graham said.

I dragged George's armchair up by the opposite side of the bed. *Anna Karenina* had been returned to the library and replaced on his nightstand with another Russian doorstop: *The House of the Dead*. I turned it so the unsettling title faced away from me and extracted the book which it lay atop: the one I loved best. Comforted at its familiarity, I hugged it. It was taking us far longer than usual to get through it this time.

For a while the two of us sat there, me hugging *Zenda*, both of us watching George.

"Want me to read to you?" he asked.

So, all through that long night vigil, it was me curled up in the armchair on one side of George, and Mr. Graham's pleasant voice on the other side of George, and Rudolf Rassendyll and Princess Flavia coming to life in the space between, where George lay silent as a corpse as I drifted in and out of dreams.

A U G U S T *19*, *1927*: F R I D A Y

*I*n the early morning, Lindbergh woke me, pawing at the skirt of my nightgown. I let him down in his basket so he could do his business, watching as he bounced around sniffing everything and letting out a bark or two before jumping back into the basket to be brought up again. He immediately returned to George's bed to keep an eye on him.

Wide awake now, I settled back into the armchair. Mr. Graham was quite dead asleep across from me in an incredibly uncomfortable-looking hunch.

"Hey, Lou."

The hoarse whisper startled me, and I gazed at George, awash with relief that he was awake and speaking. I scooped up the kisses from the nightstand and dumped them within reach of his good hand, settling back into my chair.

"A kiss for you," he said, tossing me one. His aim was off, but I caught it.

"They're for you," I protested, secretly very pleased, as it might be the only kiss I'd ever get out of George. "Because I'm sorry for all the trouble I've made for you."

"Aye, nae bother," he said, and I couldn't help but laugh, softly. He laughed too, but apparently it hurt him, and he stopped abruptly with a wince. "I don't suppose you could rustle up some water?" he said. "I think I swallowed the Gobi in my sleep."

"Of course," I said, eager to devote myself to his service. (For a day, at least.) As I stood up, his bedroom door opened, and Mrs. Graham stood there, looking like a frazzled ghostie.

"Good morning, George, how are you?"

"Stiff," Mr. Graham said, startled out of sleep and making faces as he unfolded himself.

"Not you, George," she said, waving him off as she crossed to George the Younger and dropped to her knees beside his bed, clasping his free hand to her face. He didn't protest when she kissed him, and her voice trembled as she poured out an avalanche of endearments on him. "I've made tea and chocolate biscuits, and raspberry danish, and if you're feeling well enough to come down, there's a quiche almost ready to come out, and if you don't, I'll bring some up to you—"

"Did you sleep at *all*, Alice?" Mr. Graham murmured. His eyes were closed again. She ignored him and went on.

"I think you should come down. You can rest on my bed," she told George. "Then you don't have to be all by yourself all day while your father's at work."

"Alice, you're brutal," Mr. Graham moaned.

"You missed an entire day yesterday," she reminded him. "I'm fine." She got to her feet and held out a hand to me. "Come on, Louise, let's let George get himself up and convince his father to bring him down—"

"I HAVE feet of my own!" George called after us. I couldn't help laughing, and Mrs. Graham surprised me by pulling me into a hug halfway down the stairs.

It was over and she'd moved on within seconds, but it spoke volumes about how she was feeling.

I think those Russian writers George is currently so obsessed with could take a cue in Effective Brevity from Mrs. Graham.

AUGUST 20, 1927: SATURDAY

*A*side from a lingering headache and a few days of being unsteady on his feet, George was all right again almost at once. Oh, and his arm hurt a lot, although he wouldn't admit it. (Why ARE boys so stubborn?)

Getting dressed was a nuisance, and Mr. Graham had to help him in the bath because he couldn't manage washing his hair with one hand, and he wasn't supposed to get his cast wet. Poor George. He did so hate being fussed over.

Except for getting absolutely spoiled with all the best food Mrs. Graham could dream up. He seemed oddly unbothered by *that* kind of fussing.

Mother came to see me this evening, in my room—before I was asleep, this time. She was in her nightgown and robe, hugging a cardboard box as she sat on the edge of my bed, biting her lower lip and hesitating several minutes before she set the box between us on the bed.

"I... have something for you," she said, lifting the flaps on the box and taking out a composition book. I recognized it as the one she's been scribbling in for months now. She handed it to me and I opened it.

The pages were densely covered in her pretty handwriting, full of crossed-out bits, re-written lines, arrows pointing from one place to another, and those little bottomless triangle things that point to words added above a line. My eyes went swimmy—not from tears— and I glanced at her in a panic.

"I know it's messy," she said, apologetically. "I just finished it last night and I didn't want to wait to make a clean copy, although I promise I will—"

It was obvious this was of great importance to her, and yet there was no way I could decipher it. I also didn't want her to leave me alone. I pushed it back to her and said, "Will you read it to me?"

There was a moment of silence as I watched her face, mentally begging her to say yes. "Please?"

At last she took the book back, and I scooted over to make room for her to sit beside me, and pulled the quilt up over our legs. She took a deep breath and began to read as I leaned against her, hugging Clotilde and closing my eyes, only to have them pop open again as I realized this was her story she was reading me.

I'm not sure if it counted as poetry (it didn't rhyme), but it was like poetry. It pulled me right in, revealing my mother's barest soul—and my father, too—in ways I'd never considered.

There were a number of things that shocked me, but the shockingest one was this: I'd had two older half-sisters and a baby brother who all died from the 1918 influenza. Suddenly I began to see that my parents hadn't always been slightly detached and reluctant to show affection. It made sense. They'd had their hearts completely smashed to bits, and I was all they had left, and I too could have been lost to them any day for all they knew.

And the other thing is, that thing Mother said to me when she thought I was asleep? *Stay angry, little one, you're going to need it?* That's what Daddy said to me right after I was born.

Sometimes Mother's tears stopped her reading, but eventually we made it to the end, and sat in silence a while as I digested it all.

Mother's upbringing had been all music, all the time. No wonder she wasn't domestically skilled. She'd been left alone in the world at her grandmother's death and had to give up a scholarship to a prestigious music school to marry Daddy, so she'd have a roof over her head and be taken care of in return for mothering his dead first wife's children. Mother was so much more than just a church pianist, possibly even smarter about music than Uncle Jamie—and all these years I'd been completely, unkindly underrating her. Focusing so much on the things she couldn't or wouldn't do that I wasn't seeing

198

the brilliance of the things she *could*.

And the thought of all she gave up to become my mother at last brought me to tears, too. I hugged her tightly and snuffled out, "I just want you to love me. That's all I've ever wanted, and I didn't understand, but please—please—love me now."

"I always have," she whispered. "And I wanted to show it—but I felt so broken after the others died, and he—" (I knew she meant Sam)— "was so terrible, I just couldn't. I loved your father, too, and I'm still unwilling to face the fact that he's really gone. Because that thought is so lonely and I can't bear it."

"You have me," I said.

"I do have you. And you are so, so like him in so many ways."

I nestled into her, and for the first time in a very, very long time, she stroked my hair. Timidly at first, gradually weaving her fingers in and working out tangles, just like Mr. Graham had done the previous night.

"Are you sorry Uncle Jamie's already married?" I asked. The fingers in my hair froze. "Is that why you wouldn't come to Scotland with us?"

"Alice needed me," she said, evasive.

"What about Uncle Jamie, though?"

She extracted her hand from my hair and sat up straighter, quietly prim and dignified. "I respect him very much."

I gave her a Look, and her ears turned pink. "Even if he were free, Louise, I couldn't ever be with him. He's from an entirely different world, and I'm a nobody."

She *had* thought about it, then.

"You aren't a nobody," I said.

"I mean, he had to choose someone from his own stratum of society. His children will too. That's just how it is."

I pondered this. It was true Cousin Peter had his eye on some baronet's daughter, but...

"But if you'd had the chance to be that concert pianist, you might have—"

"Louise!" She cut me off sharply. The flush had spread to her cheeks. "He's *much* older than I am, and I would not have met him before he was married, even if he did have the music career he also wanted and didn't get. Life doesn't always give you what you think you want."

I bit back a smile. I had my answer. She was unquestionably besotted with the Unattainable Earl of Inverlochy—or at least the idea of him. I snuggled in closer to Mother once more and thought surely there must be someone available who was worthy of her—of my mother who deserved all the happiness in the world with a man who loved her.

She relaxed a little. "I just want you to know that you—having you—has been worth everything else I had to set aside. I'd do it all again, for you."

I squeezed her hand. "Does Mrs. Graham know about all this?" I asked, tapping the closed composition book.

"Some. Most of it, I guess. Nobody else—except you, now."

"Could we keep it that way?"

"I'd prefer if we did. But it's yours to share if you ever choose to."

I didn't think I ever would. Perhaps George, someday. A faraway someday.

"Why are you telling me all this now?"

"At first I was writing it for me," she admitted. "It made your father seem closer. But... after I could have lost you the other day... well. I needed to tell you too. Alice says... Alice says it's better to talk about things, even if only to one or two people, than to keep it all bottled up to oneself." She stood up. "And now it's late and I need some sleep."

I smiled at her, my cheeks a little stiff from dried-on tears, and she set the cardboard box beside me. "Have a look. It's all yours now. Good night."

After she left, I peeked inside, parting the excelsior to find several objects wrapped in yellowing newspaper.

The first was a framed family photograph of all six of us in the spring of 1918. I studied my unremembered siblings' faces. The baby was still too much of a baby to resemble either Mother or Daddy, but the older two girls had darker, wavy hair. They must have taken more after their mother, although the elder one had my face.

Daddy's face.

It was a very nice face on both of *them*. Perhaps it might become a nice face on me, too, eventually.

I propped up the frame on my nightstand so I could see it every morning first thing.

The second thing in the box was Daddy's Bible, the one he read from every night to us, before Sam came along and ruined everything. The edges were worn and the ribbon bookmark, faded and frayed, was still at the place he'd read from the night before he died. There was a part of one verse on the page underlined in blue pencil: *Rise up, my love, my fair one, and come away*. In the margin, in Mother's handwriting, were the words "With singing to Zion return."

For some reason that completely undid me, this mysterious, sacred message between my parents, and I fell into my pillow, hugging the book and sobbing. I wanted Daddy back *so fiercely*. But as I lay there crying I realized that, had he lived, we would still be in Junction City, and I'd never have met George.

If Mother had taken that scholarship, she would still be out east, and I wouldn't exist.

I'd do it all again, for you.

I charged across the hall and threw open George's door.

"Are you awake?" I asked the darkness.

He made an unwelcoming noise, and I went to snap on his light. He squinted, obviously displeased. "What?" he asked.

"Is it God that let my father die?"

"Of course not," he said, fumbling for the chain on his lamp.

"If he hadn't died, I wouldn't be here with you right now."

The light went off and I heard him settling back into his pillow with a huge sigh that said volumes about how much he wished I was not here with him at this moment. "Death is the enemy. God just works around it. Scram, I'm asleep."

I'd ask him to expound more later.

For now I returned to the box to lift out the last item, and I sucked in a breath. It was the earring box, the one Daddy made Mother soon after they married. I'd forgotten it existed until Mother mentioned it tonight, in her story. I lifted the lid with its beautiful inlaid *L*. The trays were empty now, but into one of them Mother had folded a note for me.

> *You're almost thirteen, and if you'd like to have your ears pierced, it can be your birthday treat. Either way, this box is yours now, whether you use it for earrings or other treasures. He would want you to have your turn with it.*

Other treasures. I immediately retrieved the one remaining Hershey's kiss from my windowsill, the one George threw back at me Friday morning. "A kiss for you," he'd said.

It might be the only one I'd ever get.

I tenderly tucked it into one of the compartments and reverently closed the lid, smiling.

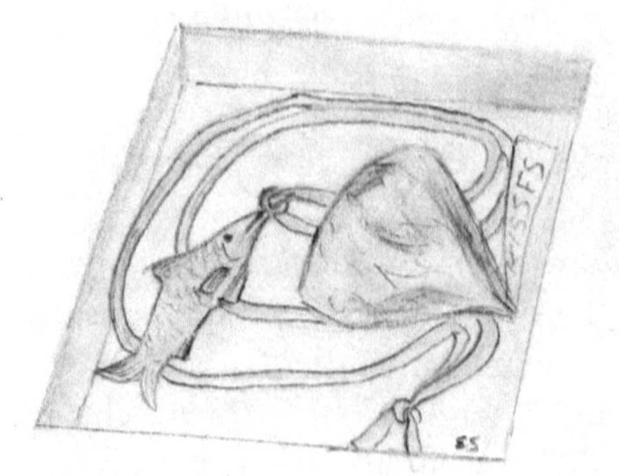

AUGUST 21, 1927: SUNDAY

George didn't go to church with Mother and me, opting to stay on the sofa in the sitting room in a pile of pillows with his eyes shut instead. Despite his bravado about having feet of his own, we could all tell he really wasn't up to walking to and from church and having to be upright on a pew for hours.

When Mother and I got home, George had *The House of the Dead* on his lap, but it was closed, and he informed me forlornly as I sat down beside him that reading made his head ache. I don't think I'd ever seen the Puppy Eyes have such intense puppy-ness before.

We were just clearing up from lunch when Officer Ferguson came to pay us a visit, saying he had news for us. Mr. Graham gave him the armchair in the sitting room and called Mother and me in from where we were washing dishes.

"Did you find who did this?" I asked Officer Ferguson, before he had a chance to open his mouth.

"We did." He took a photograph out of his pocket and handed it to me. I took one look and tossed it to the floor, turning away.

"What is it?" Mother asked, stooping to retrieve it.

"Hank," I spat out.

She saw for herself and wilted down onto the piano bench. "I was afraid it might be him," she breathed. "But Mr. Graham has been trying to locate him and his brother since March and he was nowhere to be found."

Mr. Ferguson pocketed the photograph again. "Well, he's not going to bother you any more. He's dead."

There was silence for a moment, and then Mother shocked me. By LAUGHING.

Not just a giggle.

A genuine, deep, lit-up-her-entire-face LAUGH.

I could not once in my entire life remember her ever laughing like that.

Officer Ferguson pulled out his notebook and flipped through it until he found a folded piece of paper, which he didn't hand to us just then. "We asked the Crystal Gardens for a list of their employees, and it turns out they hired a janitor named Henry Patterson in the spring, but they fired him a couple of months later when another employee caught him peeping on the dancer girls in the changing room through a hole in the closet door. They gave us his address, which was the house of a Mrs. Gladys Johnson, née Pearson—an elderly lady, widowed last year. A great-aunt, I believe. She was going senile, and he would come visit her any time her nurse was out, and nobody thought anything of it when she would prattle on about 'little Henry coming to visit me'. Turns out she was very fond of gardenia perfume and everything in her desk smelled like the stuff. That's where he nicked the papers he used."

He looked down at his notes again. "We put two men nearby on watch to see if they could catch Hank coming or going, so we could question him. In the meantime, we found out that warehouse you were in is a Pearson property, abandoned on purpose so nobody thinks it's still in use. For liquor storage. So we knew we could get him on a charge of bootlegging, even if we couldn't prove for sure he kidnapped you. Anyway, last night our men saw Hank going into the old lady's house, minutes after the nurse left, and then another man let himself in. So they knocked at the door, and we arrested them. We got Hank in handcuffs, and the other man introduced himself as Hank's brother Jim and asked us to please sit down and listen for a moment, because he had something to tell us."

"Jim?" I asked, disbelieving.

"Yes. He says he's the one who tipped off your mother back in March. He was also the one who helped Hank kidnap you. He tied you badly, hoping you'd find a way out, and planned to come back and let you out regardless. But when he got there again, you were gone, and soon Hank came along to finish what he'd started."

"Why would Jim care? He never did anything to help us before." I shuddered, thinking I'd had such a close call.

Officer Ferguson sighed. "He claims he had wanted to be out of his father's operation years ago, but had been coerced into staying. After his father's suicide, he went underground, but Hank found him and blackmailed him into helping him get rid of Louise, as per their father's instructions."

Mother reached for my hand and looked at the floor.

"Based on what you've told us, Louise, Jim's story seemed okay. But he said he wasn't interested in being given a pass out of the state to go start a new life elsewhere. He sat down and wrote this—" Ferguson held up the folded paper "—and said that it was time to pay for his sins and those of his brother. Before our men could blink, he'd whipped out a gun, shot Hank, and then turned the gun on himself. They're both dead. They won't ever bother you again."

I stared at him, automatically reaching for the note, which he put into my hand. It was a plain piece of paper, scrawled over in dull pencil.

> *Louise and Lydia I am deeply sorry for all the hurt my father and family have caused you over the years. I have been a coward and I am sorry. But I will make sure Hank never bothers you again.*

I handed it to Mother, baffled. What a silly thing for a truly innocent man to do, I thought. Maybe there was something else he figured the police would learn sooner or later.

After Officer Ferguson left, we all sat in stunned silence for about ten minutes before we started to talk it through. Mr. Graham paced, mussing up his hair again. And then Reverend Tully knocked at the door, wanting to say hello to George.

"Mrs. Pearson and Louise told me about what happened," he said. "I hope you're doing better."

"A little," George said. "And since you're here, you might as well know I've decided to be baptized."

The minister beamed at him.

"Excellent news!" he said. "When would you like to do it? I expect you won't want to wait until Easter, and you've already been through all the classes, so there's no need to wait."

"Well, I do want Mamma and Dad there..." George said, eyeing his mother as if he knew she would understand immediately.

She understood immediately. Her knitting needles flashed as she said she *had* made a promise to support George in whatever his final choice was, *even if it wasn't the choice she would have made*, and of course she wouldn't *dream* of missing his baptism any more than she'd have missed his bris, but a Jew in church on *Easter morning* was just taking it too far—

Mother's soft background piano playing abruptly silenced. George's mouth dropped open and his face went roughly the color of a raspberry.

"What's a... bris?" I asked. Mr. Graham snorted with silent laughter in his chair, also turning a weird shade of red, and Reverend Tully just stared fishlike in disbelief.

Mrs. Graham looked up, blinked at all the men, and went back to her knitting. "You're big boys, you know about these things." To me she said, "From the looks of it, you won't get an answer from either of the Georges." She cocked her head and smiled at Reverend Tully. "Perhaps you would like to do the honors, *Reverend*?"

Reverend Tully had not met Mrs. Graham before and was at a complete loss for words. Eventually he stammered, "I—I hardly think that's my place, ma'am—"

(So I asked Uncle Jamie, who never evades awkward questions, in my next letter to him.

I REGRET ASKING UNCLE JAMIE.)

That night, I lay in my bed, overwhelmed not just by the last few days but by the last several months. My window was open for the first time in ages, letting in the pleasant night air. I didn't have to worry about Hank creeping in to snatch me while I slept ever again.

I watched the shadow of Mother's earring box—*my* box—on the windowsill shift as passing cars' headlights gave it more light than the streetlight managed to do.

My year had been full of shadows, both literal and figurative. I thought about my dream, where the clouds' shadows hadn't matched the clouds casting them, and I realized all of a sudden what it meant—what I'd almost grasped, but not quite.

The reason they didn't match is because I was only seeing things how I wanted to see them. Mother, for instance, is SO MUCH MORE than I'd ever imagined. If I'd only stood back and looked, taken the time to try to know the why of her, I'd have seen that the shadow hadn't ever lied. It was my perception that was wrong.

Mr. Graham has shown me a new side of himself, too, and now I've seen it I feel I *should* have seen it all along, but I have to confess: he was always obscured by Uncle Jamie's shadow.

The thing is, Uncle Jamie is thousands of miles away.

Mr. Graham is *here*.

He's still not Daddy or Uncle Jamie, just as he himself said, but I really like him, and I'm not going to hesitate to tell him next time I have a problem I can't fix on my own.

It is a very good feeling to have adults who care about you.

And, having written all this out, I understand too why Mother wanted to write out her story.

It is so very cleansing to the soul.

208

SEPTEMBER 14, 1927: SATURDAY

A lot has happened in the last couple of weeks: getting ready for school, George arranging his baptism for October, me doing his paper route for him until his cast is off, dancing lessons... to which I am temporarily going alone.

That's the best thing, really. Being able to go out by myself without fear. Now I'm able to go look after children at their own houses, as easily as having them come to mine. I don't care how stinky or noisy they are. They're so precious I'd *almost* do it for nothing. But of course the whole point is making money for flying lessons.

Speaking of flying, Mother has finally given her (reluctant) permission for me to start lessons as soon as Mr. Graul is confident I am strong enough to manage the controls. He thinks perhaps next year. He says there's a lady named Margery Brown who's learning to fly right now (not here, somewhere else) and she's only 4' 11"! I'm already much taller than that.

So I've been shadowing Mr. Graul and Mr. Rankin every chance I get, learning all I can about engines and maintenance and navigation. Things I can do on the ground. I am in HEAVEN.

Mother's found us a house, too. It's an adorable little place only a few blocks from the Grahams', and Mr. Graham went with her to the bank so she could take out a loan. (How silly is it that she, twice widowed, can't sign her own paperwork for a loan she's going to pay back with her own money, without a man there to advocate for her?) She put out an advertisement for piano lessons and within a week she had three pupils, with several more interested. She says she has other tricks up her metaphorical sleeve as well, but I cannot imagine what they might be.

I'm just going to keep my eyes open for eligible prospective husbands for her. Not because I doubt her ability to learn to take care of herself (okay, maybe I doubt it a bit), but because it's just so unfair she should have to be all alone missing Daddy so much!!

And Susan had her babies—Robert was right, there were two! Rosemary and Stanley. She sent a telegram and Mr Graham is showing it to anyone who catches his eye as if he just won a fortune or something. It's precious. George's reaction was, predictably, to look up from his book and back down again with a polite, "That's nice, I guess."

And today—today Colonel Charles Lindbergh came to Portland, and George was well enough to come along with me to see him. (And Lindbergh's fuzzy namesake, of course.)

Once upon a time I had thought I'd want to try to wangle a ride in the *Spirit of St. Louis*, or get into a long conversation with Colonel Lindbergh, even though I'd known deep down such a thing would be impossible. The papers say he's mobbed everywhere he goes. It must be awful, never having any peace.

Mrs. Graham curled my hair for me again, and I wore the dress from Aunt Estelle (minus any Frightful Cardigans or Long Underwear, I might add), and Mother redecorated my straw hat with blue velvet ribbon and silk daisies, and I was surprised at my reflection as I put on the hat before leaving.

I... didn't look so terrible, actually.

At the airfield, I did get as close to the front of the crowd as I could to watch Colonel Lindbergh land. George's sling was useful, and he is very good at being loud when necessary. Between the sling and his melodramatic MAKE WAY, people let us pass without too much complaint. I drank in every word Colonel Lindbergh said at the airfield, and there was a parade, and he gave a speech at Multnomah Stadium, where the entire audience was made up of children and their escorts.

Aviation was the future, he said, and any one of us could help advance it if we learned to fly ourselves. I could feel all around me the excitement of boys and girls alike, who in those moments believed they could all be part of that future in the air. I wonder how many of them will act on that excitement. I hope lots of them will.

Afterwards, George and I stood by the airfield fence to watch the *Spirit of St. Louis* take off. He held my hand. It's been ages since he did that. There was an instant of cold shadow and then warm autumn sunlight again as the plane flew over us. I slouched a bit so I could lay my head against George's shoulder, eyes still riveted on the sky. The crowd began to disperse, but we didn't move.

"What'd you think?" he asked me.

"He's nice. His plane is even nicer."

"He's a bit old for you," George said, dead serious.

I burst out laughing and straightened up. "I never said I wanted to marry him!"

"Oh." He looked confused. "Don't you, then?"

Not as long as you're an option, I said. (Not out loud.) What I did say out loud was, "No, you idiot, I don't."

He looked pleased, and my heart did a little flip.

I don't need Charles Lindbergh in order to be what I want to be. I don't even need George, although I never want to be without him.

I will always have me. Louise Berglund Pearson, aviatrix-in-waiting, wants to fly.

And she will.

*M*y children, when reading a new book, always ask, "Is this a real story?" I expect most people probably wonder that, too. While Louise and George and their families are out of my own imagination, their story is shaped by what was actually happening around them at the time.

All the aviators Louise names were real aviators, including Mr. Graul and Mr. Rankin. I've ridden in a later model Waco, which is fundamentally very similar to the GXE/10 model Louise rode in, and it was a fantastic experience. They are wonderful little planes, and you can learn more at https://www.nationalwacoclub.com.

Most of what happens to Louise and George during the summer are also real events of Salem life, from the Straw Hat Day parade to the lunar eclipse to the Waco rides at the fairgrounds. Even Mrs. Frank Jones was really advertising fox terrier pups the weekend Lindbergh crossed the Atlantic.

I had to dig around a bit to learn that the significance of "Straw Hat Day" was simply the fashion world's permission to put away your winter hats for the summer; officially it's the 15th of May, not the 13th, so apparently Oregon was in a hurry that year.

The Parrish School, the one that was so overcrowded, is still a functioning junior high school in Salem today. The Leslie Junior High School that was opened in the autumn of 1927, to help relieve the crowding, moved to a new building in 1997. The original Leslie structure was razed in early 2020 as I was first drafting this story, so

I was JUST too late to have seen that building for myself! https://www.willametteheritage.org/obituary-leslie-junior-high-school-building-19 27-2020/

The "Victorian monstrosity" in which the Grahams live could be any one of a number of beautiful old houses in a neighborhood very near the current Capitol Building (the one that stood in 1927 burned down in 1935) and the Presbyterian Church, and not terribly far from Parrish School and the downtown theaters and shops that George and Louise would have frequented. I do have a particular one in mind, but I won't tell you the address. Just walk around that neighborhood if you get a chance, as I did, and pick one out that strikes your fancy.

The Crystal Gardens Ballroom is also a real place. At the time of this writing, it is being used as a church!

Charles Lindbergh (1902-1974) really did spring up out of nowhere that summer of 1927. Prior to his trans-Atlantic flight, he was just one more aviator—delivering mail, among other things. After his flight, his life was more or less a constant game of trying and failing to maintain his privacy; his goodwill tour was exhausting to him, because he was mobbed and paraded so lavishly that his real mission, to promote a love for and belief in the future of aviation, was never at the forefront.

Unfortunately Lindbergh later openly and unapologetically embraced the ideologies of Nazi Germany. In Des Moines, Iowa, in September 1941, he delivered an infamous speech for the America First Committee (you can read a transcription here: http://www.charleslindbergh.com/americanfirst/speech.asp)

Germany had been spreading propaganda for years prior to the war's outbreak, saying that the Jews were at fault for... well, pretty much everything wrong in the world, and Lindbergh's speech sparked outrage because it seemed to indicate he agreed with the propaganda. Louise, like many other Americans fighting to end the atrocities Hitler's regime was committing, will at that point be thoroughly disillusioned by this former American hero. *The Rise and Fall of*

Charles Lindbergh, by Candace Fleming, is an excellent biography of Lindbergh. If you want something more exhaustive, *Lindbergh* by A. Scott Berg is unrivalled.

(If Louise is fed up by it, just imagine what Alice will be saying.)

Thea Rasche (1899-1971) came to America in 1929 to take part in the Women's Air Derby. Steve Sheinkin has written a fantastic book about that race, *Born to Fly*, which I highly recommend. I can't help but believe a fourteen-year-old Louise will be tracking that derby with even greater excitement than she had following Lindbergh in 1927.

Dr Nathan Cohen Beskin (1877-1953) was also a real historical character, about whom I'd never have known except for the announcement in the Salem newspaper of his speaking engagement at the Methodist church. His son, Dr James E Beskin, wrote a book about his father's life, *The Jew Who Chose Jesus*—which is no longer in print, but does pop up on used book sites and ebay, occasionally for reasonable prices.

Louise's mother's story, just as she wrote it for Louise, can be read in the novella *élégie*, available as an ebook and audiobook. I hadn't originally intended it to be alluded to in this book, but it seemed like such a perfect example of the overarching theme, I couldn't resist

And that theme, to me, is that people, good and bad alike, are complicated. Sometimes you have to step away, look at them like cloud-shadows, realize they're not all they seem. Sometimes you'll be right about them from the start, and sometimes you'll learn you've judged them unfairly.

ABOUT THE AUTHOR

Eva was born in Jacksonville, Florida. She left that humidity pit at the age of three and spent the next twenty-one years in California, Idaho, Kentucky, and Washington before ending up in Oregon, where she now lives on a homestead in the western foothills with her husband and five children, two of whom are human.

ALSO BY EVA SEYLER

The War in Our Hearts (paperback, ebook, audiobook)
Ripples (ebook, audiobook)
This Great Wilderness (paperback, ebook, audiobook)
élégie (ebook, audiobook)
The Summer I Found Home (paperback, ebook)

FIND EVA ON SOCIAL MEDIA

Twitter: @the_eva_seyler
Instagram: @theevaseyler
Facebook: /authorevaseyler

To get book recs, news, and the occasional cat photo, consider subscribing to Eva's email newsletter here: https://www.evaseyler. com/index.php/contact-eva-seyler/subscribe-to-newsletter/